Darkened Streets

By

Wayne Phillips

Disclaimer

This book is a work of fiction. All characters, names, locations and situations appearing within are products of the author's imagination. Any resemblance to real-world equivalents is unintentional and purely coincidental.

Table of Contents

Copyright Page 1

Prologue 5

Chapter 1 16

Chapter 2 22

Chapter 3 28

Chapter 4 33

Chapter 5 39

Chapter 6 46

Chapter 7 56

Chapter 8 62

Chapter 9 68

Chapter 10 79

Chapter 11 89

Chapter 12 94

Chapter 13 102

Chapter 14 107

Chapter 15 113

Chapter 16 121

Chapter 17 129

Chapter 18 136

Chapter 19 144

Chapter 20 150

Chapter 21 157

Chapter 22 161

Chapter 23 168

Chapter 24 175

Chapter 25 181

Prologue

Gavin Powell looked up in surprise as his computer screen began to flicker on and off. In the hallway the same thing was happening to the lights. During the four years he had worked at the army research centre, nothing like this had ever happened before and he was immediately concerned. This strange phenomenon continued for a few moments more, then suddenly the room went dark.

Gavin held his breath and counted in his head while he waited for the emergency generator to kick in. When he reached ten without the power returning, he stood up from his desk and went to the window. He pulled aside the thick curtain and was momentarily blinded by the sudden influx of light. It was late on Friday afternoon, and within half an hour the sun would set.

His office was on the second floor, affording him a clear view over the surrounding landscape, even though there wasn't much to see. The bare, flat plains of the Carlton Desert seemed to stretch endlessly in every direction. A few sparsely scattered trees somehow made the land look even less hospitable. Far in the distance, Gavin could barely make out the control tower at the abandoned airport. Further south and beyond what he could see was the city of Carlton itself.

The base was surrounded by a three metre high chain-link fence, topped with razor wire. Normally the fence would be electrified too, but with the power currently off that was no longer the case.

The only safe way in and out of the compound was through the main gateway, which was large enough that even the massive army trucks could enter without difficulty. Like the rest of the fence, the gates were heavily fortified. They were briefly opened when vehicles arrived and left, but at all other times remained tightly shut.

A small building beside the front gate served as the guardhouse, but also contained equipment used to generate and transmit an electro-magnetic field through the perimeter fence. The field generator drew its power from a different source than the rest of the base, so even with the electricity off everywhere else, it remained active.

As he looked through the window, Gavin noticed some movement by the guardhouse. Three soldiers were locked in a heated discussion. After a few moments they seemed to come to a decision. The men separated, each heading in a different direction. One entered the first floor of the research centre, another made for the living quarters, while the third approached a group of soldiers congregating at the entrance to the mess hall.

The sound of people rushing by his office drew Gavin's attention for a moment, and when he looked back this second group of soldiers had dispersed as well.

Gavin picked up the phone, planning to call the base information hotline, but realised even before he pressed the first digit that the line was dead. He replaced the handset. Several more technicians walked quickly but calmly past his office towards the main stairs. Gavin decided it was time to follow their lead. He stepped away from the window and let the curtain fall shut, once again leaving the room in darkness.

Before he could make it to the door he found his way blocked by one of the guards he had seen outside.

'We lost contact with the lower level,' the soldier explained. 'We've tried to raise them on the radio without result. Something serious is going on, but with the power off we can't get down there to investigate. Regulations state that if something like this happens we are to assemble at the evacuation point outside the compound, but at the moment the gate is jammed. Some of the guards are looking for tools to force it open, and the rest of us are spreading the word that everyone should gather in the front yard.' As he finished speaking, the room was suddenly illuminated by a harsh redness. The emergency power had come on.

Gavin returned to the window and opened the curtain. In the guardhouse a technician was working at a control panel, but even with the electricity restored the gate remained tightly scaled.

Gavin let the curtain fall shut then booted up his computer, intending to check the diagnostic systems to see if he could figure out what was going on. Seconds later a tone indicated the computer was ready. He stared at the monitor in horror. Two words had appeared on the screen, confirming his greatest fear.

Containment Failure.

By all accounts it was impossible, yet it was happening right before his eyes. Of all the things that could possibly go wrong, this was the worst, and what's more, he had no idea how to fix it.

He lifted the phone to his ear, hoping the line had been restored with the electricity, but was immediately disappointed. He realised the moment the creature in the basement breached its containment cell, an automatic quarantine was triggered, meaning not only was the entire complex sealed to prevent anything entering or leaving, but also that all modes of communication had been cut, except for a few secure lines which Gavin wouldn't be able to access because he was only a low-ranking technician.

He turned to the guard. 'Finish your search of the building and make sure everyone knows to evacuate. I'll go into the basement and turn off the charge to the fence. That should make it easier for the others to open the front gate. If I'm not back by then, you need to get everyone out of the complex and shut the gate behind you. With any luck, the perimeter fence will be able to keep the creature inside.'

'What about you?'

'Anything could happen down there. It might not be safe for you to wait until I return.'

Gavin didn't bother to mention that there was no guarantee he would return at all. Everyone at the base knew just how dangerous the creature was.

With nothing more to say, the two left the office. The guard continued along the corridor, intent on ensuring everyone had left the building, while Gavin headed for the main stairs.

When he reached the ground floor he looked through the lobby entrance and into the front yard of the base. Though the gate was out of view, he could see other technicians milling around, proof that the guards were yet to make any progress in overriding the quarantine.

After a fleeting pause he continued on his mission, knowing that the sooner he turned off the charge to the fence, the sooner the guards would be able to get everyone to safety.

At the entrance to the basement Gavin keyed in his access code and pressed his thumb against the scanner, then pulled open the door and held it back against the wall using a large pot-plant. If the power went off again he didn't want to risk being trapped in the lower level.

He stood for a moment on the landing, looking down into blackness. For some reason the emergency lighting had not come on down here. He flicked at the switch but there was no change.

With the small amount of light coming in through the main doors, Gavin could see an emergency kit secured to the wall. He opened it up and pulled a torch from inside, then shone the beam down the stairs. There was no sign of the creature, but that was of little comfort to him. He took a deep breath and started to descend.

Though the research centre was one of the most modern in the country, the basement still reminded Gavin of an abandoned castle. The interior was clean, almost sterile, but the air seemed stagnant, with the temperature several degrees lower than the above-ground floors. At the best of times it was an unnerving place to be, but alone in the darkness, with the creature probably somewhere nearby, it was even worse.

As he reached the bottom of the stairs Gavin's eyes were drawn to the double doors of the laboratory, where the creature would normally have been contained. However, given that the containment had failed, he had no desire to enter. Instead he hurried down the corridor to the power distribution room. He pulled open the door and stepped inside.

In front of him were half a dozen control panels, but with the basement power offline none of them would be of any use. Instead Gavin approached a bank of levers on the far wall. He quickly found the manual override for the perimeter fence charge and turned it off. Now it would be much easier for the guards to open the gate.

With his job in the basement complete, Gavin returned to the stairs so he could leave the base with everyone else, but as he passed the laboratory a sound from inside caught his attention.

Gavin was torn. The technicians and soldiers in the basement had surely evacuated already. The noise he had heard was most likely to be the creature. On the other hand, if it was a person, they would probably need his help to escape safely.

His choice made, Gavin pushed open the double doors to the lab and panned the light from side to side as he looked for the creature. He couldn't see any sign of it.

Satisfied that it was safe to proceed, he stepped through the doors and let them swing shut behind him.

On the far side of the room several corridors led to other laboratories located under the surrounding buildings. Gavin guessed that when the power went off the soldiers and scientists realised the creature was no longer contained, and so escaped to another section of the base. Still, he knew he had to do a proper search to ensure everyone had made it out.

The lab was large, at least twenty metres square, with computers and research equipment taking up most of the space. One side of the room consisted of a mess of bookshelves, and in the centre of the opposite wall stood a metal cage, stretching from floor to ceiling, five metres wide and seven metres long, where the creature should have been.

Gavin approached the cage first. It was made of thick metal bars, like a prison cell, but between the bars was a thin wire mesh. This mesh also made up the floor and ceiling of the enclosure. Gavin knew it wasn't the bars that held the creature inside, but an electro-magnetic field running through the mesh.

The creature was unique among all animals on the planet. Aside from being mostly transparent, it was also capable of passing through solid objects. One of the only ways to confine it was within an electro-magnetic field. Unfortunately, when the power failed, the field within the mesh had been disabled, allowing the creature to escape, and now the only thing stopping it from wreaking havoc in the outside world was the stronger electro-magnetic field still running through the base's perimeter fence.

Finding nothing of interest in the cage, Gavin moved away and began searching the rest of the room. He made his way between each row of benches, carefully checking under all the tables, intent on finding anyone who hadn't managed to flee. It didn't take long for him to complete his examination, and soon the only part left to explore was the library.

The bookcases were arranged in a haphazard manner, which in the dark could be worse than a maze. He had been saving them for last because from outside it was impossible to catch even a glimpse of what lay within. It was likely the creature had escaped to the surface as soon as the power failed, but there was also a chance it was still hiding somewhere in the shelves or in a different section of the basement.

Steeling his nerves, Gavin crossed into the first row of bookcases, shining the beam of light first one way then the other. As before, he saw no-one. Moving further into the shelves, turning a corner and crossing several more rows, he was well aware that the deeper he went the more difficult it would be to leave. The dread in his stomach was quickly becoming abject terror.

Realising he couldn't bring himself to go on, Gavin called out in a hoarse whisper. 'Is anyone still in here?'

He waited a few seconds, then cleared his throat and asked again, this time louder. 'Can anyone hear me?' He listened closely for any sort of reply, but none was forthcoming.

Gavin decided it was time to go. He knew he had done as much as he could.

He turned abruptly, but in his haste to leave he struck his leg on a trolley stacked with books. A wave of pain passed over him and the torch slipped through his fingers. The light died the instant it hit the floor and Gavin heard it roll away, probably under one of the bookcases.

He dropped to his knees and frantically felt around for it, but his search was unsuccessful. Extending his arms as far as possible he explored below the opposite row of shelves, however this was no more fruitful than his previous effort.

A noise from a corridor on the far side of the room made Gavin stand. He knew right away it was the creature. It must have been in one of the other sections as he searched the laboratory. Perhaps it was returning because it couldn't find a way out.

In Gavin's opinion there were two possible courses of action. He could make a run for it, and risk piquing the creature's interest, or he could stay in the bookshelves and perhaps it would pass him by. Of course, if it did become aware of his presence, he would be trapped. He had a nasty feeling that if he stayed where he was this is exactly how things would play out. He decided to make his escape before that could happen.

He started back towards the main workspace of the laboratory but quickly came to a stop. Instead of leaving the library, he found himself deeper than ever. He realised in his scramble for the torch he had gotten turned around.

Returning to the row he had just left, Gavin was suddenly aware of something under his foot. A moment later he lay on his back staring up at the darkened ceiling. He hoisted himself into a sitting position, pawing wildly in front of himself to find what he had slipped over on.

It was the torch.

He picked it up and switched it on. The beam hit him right in the eyes. He turned the light off and waited for the spots dancing in front of him to disappear. As soon as they did he turned the torch on again, this time pointing the beam down between the bookcases. He climbed to his feet. With little more than instinct to guide him, he managed to make his way clear of the bookshelves.

Before he could reach the exit he heard a faint shuffling coming from behind. He turned quickly, shining the light in the direction of the noise. For a moment he saw nothing, then it was as if the darkness itself leapt out at him.

Gavin hurled himself through the double doors and towards the stairs. He slipped a little on the first step but didn't slow down. Fear burned in his chest as he half-ran, half-stumbled to the first floor. He glanced out the front entrance but couldn't see anyone. He assumed the soldiers had prised the main gate open, allowing everyone to evacuate.

He was tempted to run towards it, but realised if the guards had followed his advice they would have shut the gate again in order to ensure the creature didn't leave the complex.

Gavin continued up the stairs to the second floor. When he reached the landing he risked a glance behind. The creature didn't seem to be following anymore.

As he arrived back at his office, Gavin heard people start to scream. He realised then that the other technicians hadn't managed to escape; they had just been out of sight as he returned from the basement.

He rushed to the window and pulled aside the curtain. Harsh afternoon sunlight once again poured into the room. One storey below him his worst fears were coming true. The creature was prowling back and forth just inside the main gate, confined within the complex by the electro-magnetic field running through the external fence.

Most of the people were already fleeing into the research centre or around the back of the building, but several were frozen in place, apparently too scared to move.

Gavin watched in horror, knowing that sooner or later the creature would turn on those nearby. The only way to save everyone would be to let it out of the compound.

The gate was sealed, but if he could shut off the field generator, the electro-magnetic field would fail and the creature could pass through the fence and escape into the desert.

Knowing he could do nothing more from his office, Gavin ran along the corridor, down the stairs, through the main entrance and into the facility's front yard. The creature was still there, as agitated as ever, but Gavin ignored it and headed straight for the guardhouse. He set his sights on the enormous electrical socket in the far corner of the room.

There was no switch to turn off, so he braced his feet against the wall and pulled at the cord. For a few long seconds he struggled in vain, then all of a sudden, the plug left the outlet. The electro-magnetic field was disabled.

By the time Gavin reached the door, the creature was already on the other side of the fence. The people in the yard began to look over at him and cheer, though he felt anything but triumphant.

In the south, beyond the barely-visible airport control tower, was the city of Carlton. With cold certainty, Gavin knew that was where the creature would go. He had saved ten or more people by releasing it, but placed thousands of others in danger.

Chapter 1

Eighteen year old Manny Logan looked slowly over the deserted college campus then checked his watch. It was already past five o'clock. Ordinarily he would never have stayed so late, especially on a Friday, but he was working on an anatomy paper and didn't have the required information at home. Fortunately he'd found what he needed at the library and could now finish the project without too much trouble.

He ran a hand through his short black hair, which still somehow managed to be unkempt. It didn't matter; that was the way he liked it. His dark hair and brown eyes he had inherited from his father, but that was about it. His clear skin had come from his mother and to an extent so had his build, but where she was the very epitome of stunning femininity, his flexible, compactly-muscled form spoke of strength and speed. Though he hadn't been in a real fight for years there was no doubt in his mind that he could hold his own if the need arose.

He wore black long pants and a dark blue zippered jacket, supposedly waterproof but actually not, left open at the front to reveal his only white T-shirt. All the other clothes in his wardrobe were dark. On his feet he wore a pair of light yet durable boots. He could move so freely in them that they seemed more like running shoes. A tattered backpack hung from one shoulder.

In the west the sun was drawing ever-nearer to the horizon. The clouds were already tinged faintly orange. Classes had finished over an hour ago and most of the students were long gone, but on the university oval across the street a few had remained behind to kick a soccer ball around.

As Manny watched the game, he heard the door behind him open and turned to see who it was. All he could make out was a girl with her head in a book and several more in her hands. Before he could move out the way, she bumped into him, immediately dropping everything she was carrying.

Manny couldn't help but stare.

Her skin was pale, perfectly complementing her sparkling blue eyes and apologetic smile. Her hair fell just below her shoulders, and though it was as dark as his, it seemed to shimmer in the late afternoon sunshine. She wore a blue blouse and a comfortable pair of jeans.

She was obviously a college student, though Manny guessed she was new. He would definitely have remembered if he'd seen her before.

Quickly she bent to retrieve her books. As Manny knelt to help, she met his gaze. 'Sorry about that. I guess I wasn't watching where I was going.' She stood up and brushed some non-existent dirt from her shirt, then held out her hand. 'I'm Grace Chambers.'

Manny took her hand and shook it warmly. 'Immanuel,' he said, 'but most people call me Manny.' He offered Grace the rest of her books. 'That's quite a haul you have there. What are you studying?'

'Architecture. The course was cancelled at my old school so I came here.'

'That's their loss, I guess,' Manny said amicably. He indicated one of the thicker books she was holding. 'I didn't know you needed to learn astronomy for architecture.'

'Actually, that one's just for me. I like to have it around in case I get a spare moment.' She laughed ruefully to herself. 'So far that hasn't happened. Dealing with the transfer has kept me pretty busy.'

'But you're free now?'

Grace regarded him curiously. 'What do you have in mind?'

'I was planning to go stargazing at the abandoned airport with a friend of mine. It's one of the few worthwhile activities you can do for free in this town. You're welcome to join us if you like.'

'As long as you don't want to stay out too late.'

'Just an hour or two.'

'Are you leaving now?' Grace asked.

'Soon,' Manny said. 'I'm waiting for my friend. Carla Morgan.'

The name seemed familiar to Grace. 'Does she go to school here?'

'That's right. She's studying engineering.'

'What about you?'

'I'm a medical student.'

Grace was surprised. 'They have that here?'

'Yeah. It's only a small campus, but the resources are first-rate. A lot of people come here specifically for the medical program.'

Across the street the soccer game had reached its end and the players were starting to drift away. Manny checked his watch. 'I guess Carla's running a little late,' he said apologetically.

Grace took a seat on a nearby bench and set her books down, apparently content to wait with him. Manny let his backpack slide to the ground then sat beside her.

He looked around, his eyes coming to rest on the entrance to the college parking lot. He realised that must have been where Grace was going before she ran into him.

'You're not staying in the student accommodation, are you?' he asked. The student accommodation consisted of several dorms just around the corner, close enough that Grace wouldn't need a car.

'No. I have an apartment a few blocks west of here.'

'You're probably not too far from me,' Manny said. 'I live with my mother. She's a nurse at the hospital. My dad works at the mine on the other side of the mountains, so we only see him every few weeks.'

'You're lucky,' Grace said. Off Manny's confused look, she added, 'Living with your family. This is actually my first time away from home. I've been here a week, but I'm still not completely comfortable being on my own.'

'You have nothing to worry about. The people here are friendly and there's very little crime. In fact, Carla's father is on the police force. Her family moved in a few doors down when I was about five. That's how we met,' Manny explained.

He glanced down the street as a black jeep came around the corner. 'That looks like Carla now,' he said. He stood up and helped Grace to her feet, then retrieved his backpack.

'I'll get my car and follow you, that way you can stay later if you want,' Grace said. 'I'll only be a minute or two.' She started towards the parking lot as the jeep pulled up at the curb.

It was a two-seater, with an open-air cab and enough room in the tray to fit one or even two people if necessary. At the moment however the space was filled with a picnic basket and a telescope, as well as the jeep's canvas canopy which could be set up if it started to rain. Manny added his backpack to the pile, then opened the passenger side door and climbed into the vehicle.

Carla sat in the driver's seat, her blonde hair pulled up in a loose ponytail. With one hand she held the steering wheel, while the other rested on the door of the jeep. She wore long sleeves, but had them bunched up near her shoulders. Her face was hidden in the shadows of an old baseball cap, making her green eyes appear even darker than normal.

Though the jeep belonged to Manny, it was common to find Carla behind the wheel. She had her own car – a second-hand convertible – but most of the time she was with Manny and it was more convenient for them to share his jeep.

Carla watched Grace disappear around the corner of the building, then turned to Manny. 'Who was that?' she asked.

'Grace Chambers. She's new here and likes astronomy so I invited her along. That okay?'

Carla shrugged. 'Fine by me. Does she know how to get there?'

'Her car is in the student parking lot. She'll be out in a few minutes and then she'll be able to follow us.'

Carla looked in the mirror and adjusted her earrings. 'She seems nice.'

'You mean you've met her?'

'Earlier in the week. She needed directions to the library. Nice girl,' she said, then nodded as if agreeing with herself.

Manny regarded her thoughtfully for a moment, feeling as though he was missing something, but before he could think too much about it Grace's car appeared behind them.

'And we're off,' Carla said, pulling into the street.

They left the city centre and entered the industrial district. Storefronts and public buildings were quickly replaced by warehouses and factories.

In the past, manufacturing had been a major part of the town's economy, but those days were long gone. Like the airport, most of the buildings in the industrial district were abandoned.

Less than a minute later the two cars passed out of the city and now there was only open desert in front of them. The areas of ground not barren were mostly covered in dying grass. A few skeletal trees brought some variance to the grim scene.

The quality of the roads rapidly deteriorated until Carla was driving on bare dirt. There were potholes all over the place and she slowed her speed accordingly.

Manny checked the rear-view mirror. Grace had dropped back slightly to avoid the cloud of dust thrown up by the jeep, but with no turns, and no other cars on the road, it would have been impossible for her to lose sight of them.

Chapter 2

By the time they reached the entrance to the airport the sun had slipped below the horizon. A chain-link fence surrounded the facility, but the gate was wide open. From there it was only a short drive to the main airport structures.

The control tower consisted of two floors, with the lower level formerly being used as an office, while the actual control room and an expansive deck were located on the second floor. A storage shed sat nearby, connected to the control tower by a thin catwalk.

Carla brought Manny's jeep to a stop between the two buildings. She tossed her baseball cap into the tray, then climbed out of the driver's seat. A moment later Grace pulled up beside her.

Manny set the radio on an easy-listening station, loud enough that they would be able to hear it while they were stargazing. He knew a bit of background music would make their time together all the more enjoyable.

He left the vehicle and collected his telescope from behind the seats then carried it up the stairs to the outside deck of the control tower. Though the eastern skyline would be blocked by the control room, the rest of the scape would be totally uninterrupted.

Carla grabbed the picnic basket from the rear of the jeep and started towards the stairs.

'You seem to have gone to a lot of trouble for tonight,' Grace said, stepping out of her car.

'This is one of the few times that Manny and I get to hang out without having to worry about college and everything else, so we try to make it count. I'm Carla, in case you forgot. We met a few days ago.'

'I remember,' Grace said. 'You really saved me that day. I had no idea where I was going. I think I may have had the map upside down.'

'Don't mention it,' Carla said. 'I'm always happy to help. Though I think if you ever want a proper tour, Manny is the guy to ask. He's lived here his whole life and knows all this town's secrets.'

She moved the picnic basket from one hand to the other. She was starting to feel peckish, and realised Grace probably was too. 'If you're hungry, just dig in. I always pack extra because Manny eats like a horse.' She stood aside, allowing Grace to ascend the stairs, then followed her up to the deck where Manny was busy setting up the telescope.

Carla entered the control room and reappeared a moment later with three old chairs. They were the only things left in the room, aside from a fire-axe in a glass cabinet still strapped to the wall, and a few control panels that were bolted to the floor. Everything else had been cleaned out years earlier. Carla set the chairs down and went to stand beside Manny.

While the other two were busy with the telescope, Grace looked around. Aside from the control tower and storage building, the only other structure nearby was a small shed sitting about thirty metres away in the direction of the front gate. Grace had no idea of its purpose, though she could see power-lines connecting it to the other buildings in the complex.

'What's that shack back there?' she asked.

'The airport used to get a lot of lightning strikes, which would knock out the electricity,' Manny explained, 'so in every storm they ended up relying on emergency power. That shed holds the generator. I guess they put it out there so that while it was being used the noise wouldn't bother the people in the office. The real power-lines between here and Carlton were taken out years ago when the airport was decommissioned, but the generator is still connected to the buildings here. Not that it would do much good to start it. Most of the cables are old and rusted, and I'm not sure they can still carry the charge.'

As Manny went back to looking through the telescope, Grace approached the catwalk which connected the control tower to the storage shed. Rust was beginning to eat away at the metal, but a quick poke with her foot convinced her it was safe. She crossed the span to the small outside deck then pulled open the door and stepped into the building.

The second level was completely empty, and through the void created for the stairs Grace could see the ground floor was the same. Windows on every wall allowed her to look out in all directions, though in each case the view was essentially the same. A thick layer of dust on the floor and the smell of mildew in the air suggested it was months since anyone had been there.

Satisfied with her examination, Grace left the storage shed and returned to the chairs Carla had set up. She took a seat and claimed some biscuits from the picnic basket then set her gaze on the horizon. Small clouds were visible there, and as she watched they appeared to be moving slowly closer.

In the middle of the deck, Manny twisted the focus knob and peered through the eyepiece of his telescope. Beside him, Carla tapped her foot impatiently as she waited for her turn.

After a minute more of trying to perfect the view, Manny stepped out of the way to allow Carla a look. There was nothing of particular interest in the field of view, only a few stars, but that wasn't the point. It was a time for them to escape from the cares and obligations of the world for a little while. They had been visiting the airport for years, ever since Manny got his licence.

For a short time immediately after it was abandoned, the airport had become a sort-of party-central for the college students, but that was long before Manny and Carla started to frequent it. Now it seemed the two of them were the sole visitors. Though they tried to stop by fairly regularly, work and study often prevented it, and they were only able to manage it about once a month.

Despite the fact the sun was gone and night had set in, the temperature was still warm, though it would fall sharply within the next few hours. Manny looked over at Carla. She had pulled her sleeves down and didn't look cold, but as the night wore on that was sure to change. He glanced at Grace. Like Carla, the thin material of her shirt would give little protection against the coming chill. He made a mental note to leave the airport before the temperature dropped too much.

Manny left Carla's side and walked halfway down the stairs. From that position he was able to see through the windows into the office area under the control room. Inside were several desks and chairs, and even a few old computers.

He continued down to the ground and tried the door. It was secured by a chain and padlock, which would have kept any prospective thieves out immediately after the airport closed, but now, five years later, time and rust had turned the restraints into only a small obstacle. In fact the entire facility, from the buildings to the runways, and even the external fence, was in a state of general to horrendous disrepair.

'They left a lot of stuff behind when they deserted this place,' he said, more to himself than Carla. 'Maybe one day we should come back here and take anything worthwhile. It's not like anyone would care.'

Carla looked up from her position at the telescope. 'The only thing I'm interested in is the emergency generator. Imagine the power that that thing would give off.'

Manny laughed softly to himself. 'It's bolted to the floor, and even if you could get it free, you'd need a forklift and a dump-truck to get it where you wanted it.'

Carla laughed too. It was infectious. 'A girl can dream.'

'Does it even still work?' Manny asked.

'It does. I came out here with Cameron a few weeks ago and we got it running.' Cameron was a friend of Carla's, and he shared her passion for engineering. 'We had to replace the fuel, but other than that it was in perfect working order. I was a little hesitant about starting it, considering it's still connected to all the old power cables around here. I thought it might short-circuit or something, but it all worked fine.'

Carla stepped away from the telescope and hugged herself as a cool wind blew in across the desert. She poured two cups of coffee from the thermos and offered one to Manny when he arrived back on the deck.

As Grace took her turn at the telescope, Manny settled onto one of the chairs beside Carla and they started discussing the week gone by.

Chapter 3

Manny checked his watch, surprised to find they had already been stargazing for over two hours. He was sitting on one of the chairs but would occasionally take a short walk around the buildings or look through the telescope, though most of the time he was content to sit and talk with Carla and Grace. He hadn't felt so relaxed for a long time.

Grace sat at his feet with the picnic basket in front of her, slowly working her way through a chicken sandwich. Though she claimed to be interested in astronomy, she had spent more time digging through the hamper than she had studying the sky.

In the centre of the deck, Carla waited by the telescope, staring towards the north. 'The army base is dark tonight,' she said suddenly.

Manny stood up. 'I didn't notice. How long has it been like that?'

'I guess since before we arrived. I just didn't pay any attention.'

'Why do they have an army base here?' Grace asked.

Manny shrugged. 'It's as good a place as any. The area's mostly deserted so they have as much room as they need. I guess they do drills and stuff.'

He moved over to stand beside Carla, shifting the alignment of the telescope so it was facing the base, then peered through the eyepiece. As expected, he couldn't see a thing. Though the moon was full there just wasn't enough available light. Of course, even if the base had been lit up like normal, he wouldn't have been able to see anything useful either. He had examined it on other nights, but aside from watching soldiers patrolling the perimeter, there wasn't much else going on. Obviously if anything interesting was happening there, it was happening indoors, away from prying eyes.

Manny stepped aside in case either of the girls wanted a turn. Carla continued staring in the direction of the army base with a vague look of confusion on her face, while Grace poured a cup of coffee from the thermos. Neither made a move for the telescope.

Manny checked his watch again, remembering he had promised Grace they wouldn't be out at the airport for too long.

A gust of wind blew in across the desert, emphasising just how cold it was going to become. Though he had dressed warmly, Manny could feel the cool night air slowly working its way through the sleeves of his jacket and up against his arms. He had to admit the night was cooler than he would have preferred. He shivered involuntarily.

Looking over at Carla, he could immediately tell by the way she was hugging herself that she too was feeling the chill. Her shirt, even though she had pulled the long sleeves down, did nothing to protect her from the cold.

'Would you like my jacket?' he asked her.

She shook her head. 'I'm fine.'

Manny turned to Grace. 'How about you?'

'I have a coat in my car,' she said, looking out into the desert as another gust of wind whipped her hair around her face, 'and I think that's my cue to go and get it.'

She climbed to her feet and started down the stairs. On the third step she stopped, confused, then turned back to Manny. 'Did you turn your radio off last time you were at the jeep?' she asked.

'I haven't been down there for a while.' He paused, trying to remember his most recent walk around the buildings. 'I'm not sure it was on then either.'

He left the telescope and crossed the deck. Grace stood aside and let him slip past her. With the girls following closely behind him, Manny descended the stairs and approached the two cars. He leaned over the driver's door of his jeep. Though the key was in the on position, and the radio was turned on too, no sound came out. He opened the door and slid into the driver's seat then attempted to start the engine. It struggled for a moment but then died.

Manny leaned back in the seat, puzzled. 'I guess the battery went flat.'

'From just having the radio going?' Grace asked.

'It's a pretty old battery,' Manny explained.

Carla held the door for him as he climbed out of the jeep. 'But we've done this heaps of times before and never had anything like this happen.' Already she was wondering if there was some other way to explain it. 'Maybe I left the headlights on.'

'I don't think so,' Manny said, but checked the switch regardless. It was off, just as he had expected.

'What else could it be?'

'I have no idea.'

Carla went to the front of the jeep and lifted the bonnet. The terminals on the battery seemed to have a good connection, and there were no obvious problems with the engine.

'Anything?' Manny asked.

'Everything looks normal here. Grab your jumper leads and we'll see what happens.'

Manny rummaged around in the tray of the jeep without result. 'They're not here. I guess when I cleaned the jeep the other day I took them out and forgot to put them back.'

Carla turned to Grace. 'Do you have yours?'

Grace shook her head. 'I'm pretty sure they're still at my apartment somewhere. I haven't found the time to unpack everything yet. I can go and get them if you like. It shouldn't take more than fifteen minutes.'

'I think we should all go,' Manny said. 'I'm not totally sure where mine are, and if you can't find yours we may have to use Carla's.'

'That's probably a good idea,' Carla agreed, closing the bonnet.

Manny quickly pulled the canopy over his jeep. The storm clouds were starting to look promising, and he didn't want to risk leaving the jeep uncovered, even if only for a few minutes.

Following his lead, Carla ascended the stairs and took the seats back inside the control room, then grabbed the picnic basket. She returned to the ground and handed the hamper to Manny so he could put it in his jeep.

'What about your telescope?' Grace asked him.

He looked up at the deck as if trying to come to a decision. 'It can stay there for now. Rain won't hurt it and it's not as though anyone's going to come out here while we're gone.'

He moved over to Grace's car and held the door for her as she took the driver's seat, then he climbed into the rear of the vehicle leaving the front passenger side for Carla.

As Grace pulled away, Manny looked back at the jeep. He knew the radio hadn't flattened the battery, but had no idea what else could have done it.

Chapter 4

Minutes later, three-quarters of the way back to Carlton, Carla leaned forward in her seat and stared at something just coming into view on the road ahead of them.

'What is that?' she asked.

As they drew closer the headlights revealed a car in the middle of the road. It was stationary, without lights, and facing towards the airport.

Grace pulled over and cut the engine, at the same time looking around for any sign of the driver or something to indicate why they had stopped there.

Manny opened the door of Grace's car and climbed out. 'Stay here,' he told the other two.

He approached the stricken vehicle. The driver's door was wide open, but there was no-one in the car. He scanned the area, but couldn't see anyone in the darkness either.

'Anything?' Carla asked. She stood by the passenger side door of Grace's car, several questions already running through her head. 'What were they doing? Aside from the airport, there's no reason for them to be here.'

'Probably just out for a drive,' Manny said.

Grace wound down her window and peered out. 'What do you think happened?'

'Maybe they ran out of fuel,' Manny suggested. He checked the fuel gauge. The tank was half-full. He twisted the key. The engine tried to turn over but couldn't. 'Another flat battery,' he said, perplexed.

'The driver must have thought no-one would come by so they decided to hike to town,' Carla guessed.

'They wouldn't have left the door open like that,' Grace said, finally stepping out of her car.

Carla looked uneasily from side to side, then up and down the road. 'Grace is right, Manny. Something is going on here. I think we should leave.'

Manny ignored her. He pulled a key-ring torch from his pocket, then switched it on and began to pan the beam back and forth, checking the area to the rear of the car. Almost immediately he paused, a look of confusion on his face. He moved around the back of the vehicle towards something in the beam of light.

'What is it?' Carla called.

'Don't come over here,' Manny warned, kneeling down and disappearing from view behind the second car.

Disregarding his advice, Carla rushed to join him. 'Oh no!'

Grace quickly followed. As she arrived beside Manny, she let out a stunned gasp then clamped her hand over her mouth.

On the ground at Manny's feet was a woman. He felt for a pulse but it soon became clear his search was in vain. He laid the woman out flat then bent forward to attempt CPR and mouth-to-mouth resuscitation.

'Do you have a phone?' Carla asked Grace.

'In the glove compartment.'

Carla hurried back to Grace's car and found the phone. She dialled the emergency number and explained the situation to the operator on the other end of the line.

After two minutes of trying to revive the woman, Manny pulled away. He gently touched her cheek. It was cold, and he could tell she had been there for a long time.

'Isn't there anything we can do for her?' Grace asked.

'Nothing,' Manny answered. He opened the woman's eyes and shone the light in them. 'She's been dead a while. It must have happened soon after we arrived at the airport.'

Carla glanced around, searching for an explanation. 'What could have caused this? Was she in some sort of accident?'

Manny shrugged. 'I don't think so. There's no sign of a crash on the car. She may have had a stroke or something but that seems unlikely because she appears to be otherwise healthy.'

'Then what?'

'I don't know. All I can tell you is it must have been sudden.'

Immediately Carla became agitated. 'Something like poison? The army base isn't too far from here. It would be a prime target for that sort of thing. That could explain why no lights were on there.'

'I doubt it. The airport is directly between here and the base. If it were some sort of bio-weapon it would have hit us as well and we'd all be dead too.'

Realising he was right, Carla left his side and approached the car. 'There are skid marks behind the wheels, like she braked suddenly, but no sign of what she was trying to avoid. No other tyre marks or animal tracks. The only footprints here are hers, and judging by the spacing it looks like she was running the moment she left the vehicle. What's even stranger is that the footprints are still spread out where she fell. It's as though she died mid-stride.'

'There might have been a spider in the car. She could have started running and had a heart attack. If she left the radio or lights on, that could explain the flat battery,' Manny theorised.

'Maybe,' Carla agreed, but her voice lacked conviction. She was staring into the distance as three sets of flashing lights drew nearer. 'I asked for both ambulance and police,' she explained, 'though it looks as if the ambulance won't be required.'

While they waited for the convoy to arrive, Manny approached the woman's car and tried the key again. The engine spluttered as before then cut out completely. He shone his torch across the dashboard. The headlights and radio were both off, meaning they couldn't have drained the battery.

Manny switched off his torch as the first of the police cars came to a stop a few metres away. An officer climbed out of the vehicle and went straight to the fallen woman. The ambulance pulled up moments later, followed by the second police car.

When it became apparent that there was nothing he could do for the woman, the officer stepped out of the way to make room for the paramedics. He turned to Manny. 'What happened here?'

'We're not sure. It was like this when we arrived.'

The officer pulled out a small pad so he could take notes. 'When was that?' he asked.

'Only a few minutes ago.'

'So you don't know how long she's been here for?'

'We went out to the airport to stargaze just after sundown, and she wasn't here then, so it must have happened within the last two hours.'

'Do you have any idea why she might have stopped here?'

'There are skid marks like she braked to avoid something, but no sign of what that could have been. We figured it might have been because of something in the car – maybe a spider.'

'Did you notice anything else that might suggest a cause of death?'

'There are no wounds on her and in every other respect she seems to be completely healthy. I think the most likely explanation is that when she started running her body produced too much adrenaline, which triggered a heart attack.'

The officer nodded thoughtfully as he finished taking notes, then tucked the pad and pen away. He pulled a radio from his belt and started speaking into it.

Assuming they were done, Manny left the officer's side and went over to where Carla and Grace were watching as the paramedics used their equipment to examine the woman.

'They came to the same conclusion you did. They think it must have happened over an hour ago,' Carla said. She turned her back on the scene and looked towards the town. 'I think it's time for us to go.'

Manny continued to watch the paramedics. 'You and Grace can leave if you like. I want to stick around for a while.'

'There's nothing more you can do here,' Carla said gently.

Manny nodded and together the three of them returned to Grace's car. Before they could set off, they were approached by another police officer. 'I need to get your details,' he said, pulling a notepad and pen from his pocket. 'We may want to ask some more questions when we have a better idea of what happened here.'

Grace took the items from him. 'No problem,' she said. She wrote her contact information down on the pad and then gave it to Carla, who added her name and address to the page before passing it to Manny so he could do the same.

'We also noticed there are no lights on over at the army base,' Manny told the officer, handing back the pad and pen. 'I'm not sure if it could be related to what happened here, but it might pay to have somebody go over there to check things out, just in case there was a biological attack or something.'

'Okay. I'll make sure someone looks into that.' He tucked the pen and paper into his pocket then stepped away.

With the police officer satisfied, Grace started her car and carefully manoeuvred around the accident site, then continued towards Carlton.

Chapter 5

A few minutes later Grace pulled to a stop on the edge of the street in front of her apartment.

'Just wait here a second and I'll see if I can find those jumper cables,' she said.

Manny stretched a little in his seat then undid the seatbelt. 'I'm not really in the mood for another trip to the airport tonight. I'm pretty sure no harm will come to the jeep from spending the night there. I put the roof on, so I won't have to worry if it starts to rain. I think the best thing to do is leave it until morning. Carla and I can go out then and pick it up.'

'If you're sure,' Grace said doubtfully. Then, off Manny's look she added, 'I can give you a ride home if you like. It's no trouble.'

'That won't be necessary. It's only a few blocks.' He climbed out of the car, followed by Carla and Grace a moment later.

'I guess I'll see you around,' said Grace, still looking a little hesitant.

'I guess so,' Manny agreed.

Grace locked the car, then made her way up the concrete path. Using the porch light she found her key and unlocked the front door. Carla turned and started to walk away. Manny watched for a few moments longer until Grace was safely inside, then hurried to catch up with Carla. Grace's light went off leaving the neighbourhood in darkness. They had spent much longer at the airport and accident site than Manny intended, and now it seemed the rest of the townspeople had gone to bed.

The clouds they had noticed at the airport had continued to grow and now covered most of the sky, including the moon. The air had cooled considerably in the last few minutes.

A worried expression began to form across Manny's features.

'Maybe we should hurry home,' he suggested to Carla. 'It looks like it's about to start pouring.' He said it, not for his sake, but for hers. With his long pants and not-so-waterproof jacket he was at least partially protected from the elements. The clothes she wore gave no such favour. And yet the cool wind and the idea of rain didn't trouble her, so she shook her head minutely.

For a few moments they walked in companionable silence, then suddenly Manny stopped and turned, staring back in the direction of Grace's apartment.

'Regretting leaving your jeep out?' Carla asked.

'I thought I heard something,' he explained.

Carla followed his gaze, unconcerned. 'Probably a cat.'

He nodded slightly but didn't seem in any hurry to carry on.

Carla reached out and touched him gently on the shoulder, a comforting gesture because she knew exactly how he was feeling. 'It's been a weird night,' she said, 'and you're still a little freaked out by it.'

She would have continued, but her attention was drawn to something over Manny's shoulder. At first her face coloured with confusion. Then she froze.

Manny immediately turned.

'What is it?' he asked, unable to see anything in the darkness.

'I don't know, but it was big. At least a metre and a half tall, and maybe two or three metres long.'

As the words left her mouth, Manny saw it, and exactly what it was, he had no idea, only that it wasn't good. He squinted, trying to get a better look. It seemed to be somehow made of darkness. It was moving slowly but purposefully, and headed straight towards them.

For a moment he couldn't move. A terror unlike anything he had ever experienced flashed across him. His body wanted to stay immobile, but his mind realised that wasn't an option. Staying still wouldn't hide them from view. Whatever it was, it already knew where they were.

He grabbed Carla's hand. 'Let's go,' he said.

As they started to run, Manny glanced over his shoulder. He could barely see it, but he knew it was following them. Even worse, its speed had increased. His first instinct was to run home, but that was out of the question. His house was still a few blocks away, and he felt sure that this creature would chase them down before they covered even half the distance. Nor could he risk leading it back to Grace's house, or any other populated area of town.

On impulse, he turned down a side street, pulling Carla along behind him. They crossed out of the residential area and into the town's industrial district. Manny scanned from side to side, looking for a good place to hide.

Then, as they ran, the clouds opened. It wasn't true rain at first; more like a thick fog, a breath of moist air. Droplets hadn't yet started to form. The wind blowing in from the desert made the water feel colder than it really was, and under different circumstances it would have been almost pleasant.

But now, pursued by some unknown entity, Manny's only thoughts were of escape.

For a few moments the watery mist brushed against the two of them, then the fog condensed and rain began to fall.

Soon they were both wet from head to toe. And still the creature pursued them.

'What do you think it is?' Carla asked.

In a moment of rare clarity, Manny realised it was the cause of the accident in the desert, and it had followed them into town. 'I have no idea.'

Carla glanced behind them. 'Where is it?'

'I don't know. Close.' He didn't slow down as he answered, but he did hazard a quick look over his shoulder. He couldn't see it, but every instinct in his body told him to keep running.

As they moved deeper into the industrial district, the combination of their frantic sprint and the cold air made Manny's chest throb. He knew Carla was feeling the same, but they had no choice except to keep running in the wet darkness.

The wind speed picked up, chilling Manny to the bone as the fury of the storm increased. It was no longer like the light, easy rain that accompanied a summer picnic, but the fierce, heavy rain that would come only in the dead of night.

A bolt of lightning spider-webbed across the sky. Carla glanced back, trying to catch sight of what was chasing them. She stumbled, and only Manny's hand prevented her from falling to her knees. She had to keep her eyes on the path they were running, and trust that Manny knew what he was doing.

'Where are we going?' she called, her voice battling the wind and rain. If Manny heard, he didn't bother to answer.

Knowing neither could last much longer, he pulled her down an alleyway. With everything he had he hoped they would shake their pursuer; hoped that they wouldn't be followed.

The thickness of the dark and the heavy rain limited visibility to only a few metres in front. Manny stopped just in time to avoid hitting into a wall. He cursed himself for being so stupid. He had gone down an alley he didn't know, and now the two of them were boxed in. The only way out was back the way they had come. With no other option, Manny turned and prepared to make another run for it.

A bolt of lightning lit up the sky. He looked at Carla. Her long blonde hair had been plastered across her face and neck by the rain so that it appeared black. 'Are you ready?' he asked.

Without waiting for an answer he started to run. She didn't move with him. He turned to see what the delay was. Lightning flashed across the sky and he saw her lips moving. She was shouting with all her strength but he couldn't hear a word. He held his hand to his ear, trying to catch what she was saying as well as attempting to convey to her that there was no way to be heard above the storm. Another strike of lightning lit up the sky and she was able to see what he was doing.

She understood. She pointed up, in the direction of the wall they had nearly hit. Three metres above the ground was a platform, with a door leading into a warehouse. Manny quickly looked around, hoping to find something that would get them a little closer to the ledge. There was nothing.

Without speaking a word he knelt down and entwined his fingers. Carla placed her foot in his hands and allowed him to give her a boost. For a few seconds she dangled precariously but was finally able to pull herself up. The instant she was securely on the platform she reached down and grabbed Manny's wrist. Using her hand for support and pushing with his legs against the wall, he too was able to claw his way onto the ledge. Together they entered the cold, dry interior of the warehouse.

Manny waited at the door, no longer feeling the chill. His only concern was determining if whatever had been chasing them was still around. Through the darkness and the rain it was impossible to be sure, but he had the definite sense of something there.

A bolt of lightning struck nearby. In the instant it took Manny's eyes to adjust to the brightness, he saw something streak past the mouth of the alley. But his eyes had to be playing tricks on him, because it was transparent. He could see the road behind it as it passed. Even stranger, it seemed to run through a street sign. Manny shook his head figuring he must have been imagining things.

'There's a door here,' Carla called from the back of the room. Her tone was insistent. She still believed they were in danger.

'No need,' Manny said. 'It's gone.'

'What was it?' Carla asked, relief flooding her voice. She slowly slid down the wall until she was sitting on the warehouse floor.

'I have no idea. But I think it was responsible for the woman's death in the desert. It must have followed us back to town.'

'We need to tell my father about this as soon as possible,' Carla said.

Manny didn't bother to answer. He shut the door, thankful that the strange creature was no longer focused on them. In the brief moment he has seen it, he had gotten the impression it was distinctly troubled.

He took off his wet jacket and went to sit on the floor beside Carla, a cold cement wall at his back. He felt exhausted. If they hadn't found this safe-haven, he was certain the creature would have caught and killed them.

Carla leaned against him, combining the warmth of their bodies. The rain drummed ceaselessly on the roof of the warehouse. Manny squeezed as much water from his coat as he could, then handed it to Carla. She snuggled into it.

He wrapped his arms around his friend and felt her nestle against him. They were safe.

Chapter 6

Manny woke the next morning with the sun shining in through his bedroom window. He checked his alarm clock. It was already past eight. Though he had finally gotten to sleep around two o'clock that morning, it felt as if he had barely slept at all, which probably wasn't too far from the truth. He'd spent those six hours in a sort-of half-wakefulness, dreaming he was being pursued by some unseen abomination.

He climbed slowly out of bed, though that didn't stop his head from spinning, and made his way carefully to the wardrobe. After selecting his clothes for the day – some comfortable jeans and a loose black T-shirt, along with socks and a pair of running shoes – he grabbed his keys, wallet, phone and watch and headed for the kitchen.

As he passed his mother's room he stuck his head inside. She wasn't there. He guessed she had been conned into taking an early shift in the emergency department.

It was Manny's intention to join his mother at the hospital once he was finished with college, but that was beginning to look doubtful. In between holding down a part-time job at the local convenience store, school during the day, studying at night as well as volunteering at the hospital whenever he had a few free hours, he was starting to realise he had stretched himself far too thinly. Graduating with solid grades was becoming less and less likely. Yet he couldn't really give up any of his activities, except for the volunteer work, which he considered a necessary learning experience for the future.

Though the hospital wasn't especially large, it kept his mother and the other staff members busy. On one hand it was good because there was always some struggle to stay on top of the bills and overtime helped a lot, but on the other, sometimes days would go by without Manny and his mother catching even a glimpse of each other.

In the kitchen he grabbed a glass of water from the sink and gulped it down, all the while trying to get his thoughts in order. He considered making himself a sandwich, but quickly dismissed the idea. He was desperate to find Carla so they could try to piece together what was going on. He knew that if he did get hungry later, he could easily stop by one of the small stores dotted across the town and buy something to eat.

With a final look around the lounge room, he grabbed his jacket from a hook beside the door and left the house.

He was surprised to find Carla loitering in his front yard. She had clearly been waiting a while and he took it as a measure of their friendship that she hadn't tried to wake him even though it was obvious she was eager to talk to him too.

'Late night?' she asked, not bothering with pleasantries.

'You have no idea.' He glanced around at the vacant streets. 'Where is everyone?' Though it was now Saturday morning, the streets shouldn't have been anywhere near as deserted as they were.

'My father put the word out that a large, unidentified animal was seen in town, and advised people to stay inside where possible.'

'Unidentified? Now that's an understatement.'

'There's more,' Carla said. 'After you left us last night he decided it would be a good idea to call in the army. They offered to investigate.'

'I'm surprised they'd put so much stock in the words of a few college students.'

Carla shrugged. 'It's not so hard to believe, especially considering everything else that was going on last night. My father asked the coroner to put a rush on the autopsy for the woman in the desert and I managed to get a peek at the report. No cause of death could be established. It's like her brain just shut down. The army have called in some specialists to take a closer look.'

'They took over fast.'

'Faster than you think. We've already been drafted.'

'What do you mean?' Manny asked.

'They heard about our part in what happened last night, and now they want to talk to us.'

'When?'

Carla checked her watch. 'About half an hour ago.'

'You should have woken me.'

'No. I know how I felt when I woke up and I figured you probably got less sleep than me. Anyway, I'm sure it won't hurt them to wait a little while.'

'Have they set up in town somewhere?' Manny asked.

'Yeah. On the college oval. According to my father, they've erected dozens of tents there, and the whole thing is surrounded by a chain-link fence topped with razor wire.'

'They've done pretty well to get it ready so quickly.'

'Not really. My father says there have been trucks pouring into the city since about midnight.'

Manny stretched a little and yawned, at the same time glancing back towards the house. He was surprised to see his jeep parked in the driveway.

'Did you go out to the airport this morning?' he asked.

Carla was puzzled for a moment, but then saw him looking at the jeep. 'No. My father must have had one of his officers bring it back.'

Manny pulled the keys from his pocket. 'I guess we shouldn't keep the army waiting any longer,' he said, moving over to the jeep and climbing into the driver's seat. He waited for Carla to join him, then started the engine and began heading for the centre of the city.

After two minutes of driving in companionable silence, Manny turned the corner and caught his first view of the army's temporary headquarters. The scene was just as Carla had described; a city of tents inside a dangerous-looking fence. The street was lined with army vehicles and more still were parked inside the compound. Spectators were gathered around the main gate, directly across from the college.

Manny pulled into the first vacant parking space he could find. Together with Carla he left the jeep and started down the sidewalk. When they reached the gate they pushed through the crowd and tried to catch the attention of one of the imposing-looking guards. Finally a soldier with a clipboard seemed to realise they were more than average townspeople.

'Can I help you?'

'We have an appointment,' Carla explained.

The guard checked the clipboard in front of him. 'Names?'

'Immanuel Logan and Carla Morgan.'

The guard nodded. 'Follow me,' he said, leading them through the gate towards the centre of the oval. Soon they came to a collapsible table and chairs sitting in a gap between tents.

'Wait here,' their guide instructed Manny, directing him to take a seat. The soldier led Carla further into the camp.

Realising it might be a while before the other two returned, Manny began to go over in his mind the events of the previous night – from the time they had left the airport, discovering the accident, their encounter with the creature, until he finally arrived back at his house after seeing Carla safely home and explaining everything to her father.

It was the same line of thought that had kept him up for most of the night. But as much as he wondered about it, he still couldn't figure it all out. Maybe the army would be able to fill in the gaps.

Carla reappeared about fifteen minutes later, trailing behind the same man she had followed away. She smiled briefly at Manny as she was led back towards the gate. After two minutes the guard returned and motioned for Manny to accompany him deeper into the camp.

When they reached the centre of the oval the soldier ushered Manny inside a tent then closed the cloth door behind him. Manny guessed the guard would be waiting outside for the duration of the interview.

The tent was sparsely furnished. Aside from a desk and two chairs, the only other piece of furniture present was an easel holding a map of the town. Already marked in coloured pen were the location of the accident from the previous night, the airport, the military base and a line which Manny guessed traced the approximate route he and Carla had taken while trying to evade the creature once they had arrived back in Carlton. He assumed it was either Carla or possibly her father who had relayed that information to the army.

Though the map was perhaps the most interesting item in the room, Manny's gaze was quickly drawn to the man sitting behind the desk.

He was well into his fifties, with a strong face and a powerful build. He wore camouflage fatigues, like the soldiers outside, but the insignias on his shoulders indicated he was high up in the military. His nametag read "Colonel Markham".

The desk in front of him was bare apart from a few pens and a notepad. All in all, the location reminded Manny of a police interrogation room, and he wondered if it had been arranged that way intentionally.

Already feeling uncomfortable, Manny took a seat in the remaining chair.

The colonel regarded him silently for a moment, clearly trying to intimidate him.

'I hope I didn't keep you waiting long,' Manny said uneasily.

The colonel ignored him and instead picked up a pen. 'Tell me what happened last night. Start at the beginning. Don't leave anything out.'

Manny took a deep breath and began his story. 'Some friends and I went out to the airport to look at the stars. We were there for about two hours. At some point we realised the lights were off at the army base, which is pretty unusual. We decided to leave but my jeep wouldn't start, so we all returned to Carlton in another car. On the way we discovered the accident.'

He paused for a moment as the memories of what they had discovered came flooding back to him.

'At first we thought the area was deserted, but then we found a dead woman nearby. We called Emergency, and as soon as the police and ambulance arrived we returned to Carlton. When my friend Carla and I were walking home from where we had been dropped off we realised something was following us. It was too dark to get a good look, but we could tell it was big. We started running and managed to escape into a warehouse. I saw the creature run past, and I swear, it seemed to be transparent. And there's something else too. I'm sure it passed through a street sign.'

The colonel was taking notes and didn't seem at all surprised by Manny's assertion, so he continued with his story.

'After waiting for a while in the warehouse to make sure it was gone, we made our way to Carla's house. Her father is a police officer, so we told him everything. He said he'd put more men on the streets, but after I left he decided to call you guys. I suppose that's about it.'

Colonel Markham jotted a few more notes on a pad in front of him. He reread what he had written then looked up at Manny.

'How often do you and your friends stop by the airport?'

Manny shrugged. 'Roughly once a month for the past few years. That's Carla and I. Last night was Grace's first time.'

'The airport has quite a reputation. College students seem to think it's okay to go there and make trouble.'

'Maybe a few years ago, immediately after it closed, but not anymore. As far as I can tell Carla and I are the only people who still visit it.'

The colonel nodded absently, jotted down a few more notes and then turned his gaze once more to Manny.

'Were you and your friends partying?'

'We were stargazing.'

'For two hours?'

'We were talking too. Hanging out.'

'Were you drinking?'

Manny was vaguely surprised by the question. 'We weren't.'

'I read the police report. Your friend Carla made the distress call, and when the police arrived, even though the circumstances were suspicious, the three of you were allowed to leave. None of you were tested for alcohol consumption. In fact, there's no evidence the police investigated you at all.'

'Are you implying that we could have been responsible for the accident?' When Colonel Markham didn't respond, Manny continued, 'The reason we weren't considered as suspects was because there was nothing at the scene to suggest any sort of foul play. No damage to the car, no other tyre tracks, and the only set of skid marks belonged to the car in question. Though I didn't know it at the time, obviously she saw the creature and braked to avoid it. She probably panicked, causing her to have a heart attack.'

But with those words, Manny realised it couldn't have happened like that. Carla had clearly told him an autopsy had been done, but that no cause of death could be established. If the woman had died of a heart attack, there would have been signs. Manny started to wonder. Had the creature done something to the woman? There were no outward wounds, meaning she hadn't been clawed, and no broken bones or internal injuries, meaning she hadn't been crushed or thrown by it. But something like a poison wouldn't necessarily show up in an autopsy. Especially if it was a never before encountered poison from a never before encountered animal.

Manny put those thoughts in the back of his mind to think about later and instead focused on the scene in front of him. Colonel Markham was flipping through the pages in his notepad, perhaps comparing Manny's story to Carla's, and hadn't realised Manny's attention was elsewhere for a minute.

Finally the colonel set the notebook aside and looked up at Manny. 'You can go. We'll call you if we need anything more.'

Manny stood up and prepared to leave, his eyes once again falling on the map. He realised something. 'It started at the base, didn't it?'

Colonel Markham carefully scrutinised him, probably reassessing his intelligence, but didn't say anything.

'Look at your map,' Manny continued. 'The army base, the accident site and where we saw it in town. That's a straight line, originating at the army base. Last night before I went to bed, I spent a lot of time thinking about what had happened. I remembered how the lights were off at your base and I started to wonder how that was connected to everything else. I assumed that the creature must have somehow knocked out the base's electricity on its way past, but that's not correct, is it? You had it captured, but when the power went off it escaped.'

'That's a nice theory, but the problem is, you have no proof.'

'You're the proof,' Manny said. 'Your people arrived in town within a few hours of being informed about it. And even more, you came because of the words of a few college students. The story we had to tell was so crazy no-one would believe it. The only reason you did was because you already knew it was true.'

'We came at the request of the town police force. We're here to investigate an accident in the desert and to ascertain if it's connected to an animal sighting in the city. A bear maybe.'

'It was no bear,' Manny said grimly.

The colonel leaned forward on his desk. 'You were partying, drinking, trespassing and may have been involved in a fatal road accident. The police decided not to press charges, but they could be persuaded to change their mind. You don't want that. The best thing you can do is forget what happened.' The threat in his statement was obvious. He stood up and led Manny to the door, leaving no doubt that the interview was over.

Chapter 7

As Manny left through the front gate of the compound, he expected to find Carla waiting for him. Instead, she was nowhere to be found and his jeep was missing too.

He was about to call her to see what was going on when he noticed Grace walking towards him.

'What are you doing here?' he asked. Since she hadn't been around when he and Carla had encountered the creature, he knew the army would have no interest in interviewing her.

'Carla called me a few minutes ago to tell me where you were. She said she had some other things to take care of and asked if I would pick you up.' Though she was speaking to Manny, she couldn't take her eyes off the army camp.

'Did she say where she was going?'

'Not really. Something about the streets you took last night.'

Manny realised Carla had returned to trace the route they had run the previous night, obviously trying to find some evidence left by the creature. He hoped she was careful. The creature could still be around, but more immediately, the soldiers were probably doing the same thing, and Manny knew they wouldn't appreciate Carla's interference.

Unable to control herself any longer, Grace asked, 'What's going on here? Maybe I'm going crazy, but I don't remember this fence and these tents being here yesterday.'

'Last night after we left you, Carla and I were chased by some kind of animal. I'm pretty sure it caused the woman's death in the desert. It followed us for about three blocks before we were able to evade it. We told Carla's father and he called in the army.'

'For just an animal sighting?' Grace asked, confused.

'It wasn't an ordinary animal. I didn't get a good look at it while it was chasing us, but after we escaped there was a strike of lightning and I saw it run past where we were hiding. It wasn't like anything I'd ever seen before. It was like a bubble, or like water. I could see straight through it.'

Grace regarded him sceptically. 'That's not possible. The rain must have been playing tricks on your eyes.'

'My eyes were working fine, and these people know it. Why do you think they arrived here so fast? From what I can tell, they had it captured at the base but it escaped during the blackout.'

Manny paused, realising how strange it all sounded. Even looking at Grace he could tell how doubtful she was. He decided to change tactics.

'Would you like to come have something to eat with me?' he asked.

'Sure.' She surveyed the parking spaces along the side of the street. 'I suppose your jeep is still in the desert?'

'A police officer brought it back early this morning, but now Carla has it,' he said. 'I'll give her a call and see if she wants to join us for breakfast.'

Manny pulled out his phone and turned it on, but before he could dial he noticed a missed call from an unknown number. Realising it probably had something to do with the events of the night before, Manny dialled the number and put the phone to his ear.

A relieved voice came on the line.

'Manny, it's Michelle Foster. I share some classes with Carla. Earlier this morning I was in an accident on Grover Street. I think I encountered the same thing you and Carla did. I took the car to the engineering workshop at the college. Carla thought you might like to take a look.'

'Is she there with you?'

'No. I called her a few minutes ago but she was in the middle of something. She told me to get in touch with you. She gave me your number.'

'Okay,' Manny said, 'I'll be there soon.' He hung up, then quickly explained to Grace what had happened.

Together they crossed the street towards the college and headed for the engineering workshop.

A minute later they entered the garage at full speed and skidded to an uneasy stop. In front of them two guys and a girl were gathered around a jeep, similar to Manny's, but blue instead of black. They all seemed agitated, but the girl looked particularly jumpy. Manny guessed she was the driver, Michelle.

'Are you okay?' he asked.

'To be honest, I'm still a little on edge,' she said. 'Nothing like this has ever happened to me before.'

'Why don't you tell me what you saw,' Manny prompted.

Michelle started to explain. 'I was just driving along when it jumped out in front of me. It was some sort of monster. It was mostly transparent, but I could still see it. I slammed on the brakes and started to reverse. That's when I stalled the jeep. But the really crazy thing is, after the engine stopped, I swear the monster was standing inside the bonnet.'

'I had the same thought last night,' Manny admitted. 'I'm sure it passed through a street sign.'

'How could it do something like that?'

'I don't know,' Manny said, shaking his head.

'Anyway, after that I decided it would be best to make my escape on foot. I went back a few minutes later but the car wouldn't start so I called up Grady and we used his dad's tow-truck to bring it here.'

When her story was complete, Manny looked over at the jeep. One of the guys was now on his back underneath it examining the engine, while the other sat nearby with a pen poised above a clipboard.

'Are these two friends of yours?' Manny asked. As far as he knew there were no engineering classes scheduled that morning.

'Yeah. That's Grady under the car, and Ben taking notes. They're both engineering students too, so I figured they could help out. Grady started examining the car as soon as I brought it back here, just before sun-up. The only thing he could find was that the battery had gone flat.'

'What were you doing out so early?' Grace asked.

'My brother is a police officer. He told me about the animal when he arrived home from work last night. At first I thought he was making stuff up. Then my friend Amanda called and said the army had been bringing trucks into town all night, so I figured maybe Ryan was telling the truth. I decided I'd take a look around.'

Grace nodded but didn't say anything more. The whole thing seemed crazy to her, but there was no reason for anyone to lie about it.

'What do you think we should do now?' Michelle asked. 'I was considering telling the army about this. If they're going to stop it, it might help if they know where I saw it.'

'I'm not sure that's the best idea,' Manny said. 'When I talked to them, it seemed pretty clear to me that they wanted to keep this quiet. I don't think we can trust them. Plus, the creature's probably long gone by now.'

'What else can we do?'

'If you give me the address, I'll go back to where you saw it. Maybe I'll be able to find something worthwhile.'

'I'll go with you,' Michelle volunteered. 'I can show you exactly where it happened.'

'Is there anything I can do, Manny?' Grace asked.

'Until we have a better idea of what we're dealing with, the best thing you can do is go home,' he said honestly. 'I think that'll be the safest.'

Grace wasn't pleased with Manny's assessment, but she knew he had her best interests in mind. She nodded half-heartedly. 'I guess I'll see you around.'

Realising how much she wanted to be a part of things, Manny relented. 'Why don't you come over to my place tonight, say five or five-thirty. I can update you then with whatever we learn about the creature.' He pulled a scrap of paper from a nearby desk, wrote down his address and handed it to her.

As Grace turned to leave, her eyes wandered over the jeep. There was no obvious damage, nor any indication it had been in a crash, just like the car they had discovered in the desert. And that wasn't the only similarity. 'That's the third car,' she said, more to herself than Manny.

'What do you mean?'

'That's the third car that didn't start. Your jeep last night, the one on the desert road, and now Michelle's. Is it possible that the creature did something to your battery while we were stargazing? If it started at the army base like you believe, it would have had to pass right by us in order to cause the accident.'

Before Manny could think too much about it, another student entered the garage. Manny seemed to forget Grace existed as the girl, Charlotte, hurried over.

'I just heard,' she exclaimed. 'Is there anything you need me to do?'

Manny looked back at Grace as an idea flashed through his mind.

'Could you make sure Grace arrives home safely? It's not a good time for the new kid in town to be left alone.'

'No problem. Where will you be?'

'Michelle and I are going back to where she saw the creature. I'm hoping we can find something there that will tell us a bit more about it.'

With that, Manny headed for the nearest exit, leaving Grace with Charlotte. For a moment, Grace had the distinct impression Manny had deserted her.

Chapter 8

Twenty minutes later, in a car borrowed from one of the guys at the workshop, Michelle drove along an avenue in the industrial district. Manny sat in the passenger seat beside her, looking thoughtfully out the window. Though it was only mid-morning, it felt like much later in the day. He guessed it was because he had gotten such a small amount of sleep during the night.

They'd already checked the street where Michelle had encountered the creature, and even though they hadn't discovered anything useful, Manny still felt it would be worthwhile to examine the alley where he and Carla had found sanctuary the night before.

As they neared the warehouse, Manny gestured for Michelle to pull over. The moment the car stopped, he climbed out and approached the sign he had seen the creature pass through. He ran his hand over its face, checking for abnormalities, but failed to notice anything out of the ordinary.

He looked up and down the street, wondering if he should retrace his steps from the night before in case the creature had left any evidence behind as it chased them, but realised even if it had, it would probably have been washed away by the storm.

Somewhat disappointed, Manny returned to the vehicle.

Michelle waited for him to give her an indication of where he wanted to go next, but he stayed silent.

'Maybe we should try the accident site in the desert,' she suggested. 'If the creature was responsible, we may be able to find some evidence, now that we have a better idea of what we're looking for. There's no pavement outside the city so at the very least we should be able to find some footprints.'

'I don't think so. I took a pretty good look last night and didn't see anything. Assuming the woman braked to avoid the creature, its footprints should have been right there with the car, but they weren't. I still can't explain that. Maybe it has something to do with the creature's ability to pass through solid matter. Anyway, the army is probably there already checking things out. It might look suspicious if we show up.'

'Makes sense,' Michelle agreed. 'Is there anything else we can do?'

'I don't know. Maybe we'll just have to wait until someone else sees it. In the meantime, we may as well go back to the college and see if the guys looking at your jeep have made any progress.'

'Okay,' Michelle said. She put the car into gear and started the engine, but before she could leave the parking space, Manny's phone rang. He pulled it from his pocket and put it to his ear.

'You need to get to Milton Avenue,' Carla said, not even giving him time to offer a greeting.

'Why?' Manny asked, already confused.

'Just trust me,' she said, then immediately hung up.

Off Michelle's curious glance he explained, 'That was Carla. She said we should check out Milton Avenue.'

'What's going on?'

Manny shrugged. 'She didn't say, but with everything else that's happening, it's probably important.'

'I guess that settles it,' Michelle said, pulling into the street.

Two minutes later Michelle and Manny turned onto Milton Avenue. In front of them Manny could see several army vehicles parked in the middle of the street, as well as some police cruisers and two fire-trucks.

'Pull over here,' he instructed Michelle, even though they were still half a block from the action. People were gathered on the sidewalk and Manny decided it would be less conspicuous if he made his entry on foot. He worried that if one of the soldiers saw a civilian car dropping off a passenger it might draw undue interest.

He reached for the doorhandle.

'Do you want me to stick around?' Michelle asked.

'I don't think that's necessary.'

'Then I guess I'll head back to the college and see how Grady and Ben are going with the jeep.'

'Sounds good,' Manny said. 'Call me if they've found anything useful.' He climbed out of the car then started down the street.

Carla saw him approach and hurried over to meet him.

'What happened here?' Manny asked, still moving towards her.

As Carla prepared to answer, Manny passed the hedge that was blocking the site from view. It took him a moment to comprehend the destruction that lay before him.

What had once been a family home was now little more than a burned-out husk. Every surface looked as though it had been touched by fire. The corrugated iron of the roof had buckled and curled so badly from the heat that what remained of the underlying timber was clearly visible. Manny was sure the roof would cave in totally within the hour. Maybe even within minutes.

The fire responsible for the damage had obviously been both quick and savage. In all his years he had never seen anything like it. The house wasn't only burned, it was completely gutted, though by some stroke of good luck the homes on either side had remained untouched.

The family station wagon sat on its roof in the middle of the lawn, burned beyond recognition. It looked more like a pile of scrap, and if not for the awful orange paint which had somehow outlasted the flames, Manny would have had no idea it was same car he had often seen around town. There was a massive hole in the front of the garage, and he realised that's where the car had been parked before an explosion tossed it onto the lawn.

At a guess, it was the blast in the garage which had set the rest of the house ablaze, though he had no idea what could have caused the initial spark.

Manny stepped forward to get a better look at the scene. Police tape stopped his approach before he got too close. Several army officers scanned the front yard, while others collected rubble and put it in plastic bags. At the rear of the house Manny could see more soldiers doing the same thing.

Various police and fire officers stood by their vehicles on the outside of the police tape. It was comforting for Manny to know he wasn't the only one being pushed around by the army.

'When did this happen?' he asked Carla.

'Just after dawn, but I only heard about it half an hour ago. I was on my way to where we saw the creature last night, but I decided it might be a better use of my time to investigate this.'

'Do you know what happened?'

'It looks like an electrical fire started in the garage, igniting some gas bottles, which explains how the car came to be in the middle of the lawn. From there the fire spread through the rest of the house. Three people were inside at the time; a mother, father and five year old boy. Luckily the explosion woke them all and they were able to get out of the house. Fire-fighters arrived a few minutes later and did what they could. As soon as the fire was out the guys started investigating the scene, but about half an hour ago the army arrived to take over. That's when one of the fire-fighters called me.'

'Is there any evidence that the creature was here?'

'The fire-fighters didn't find anything, but that doesn't mean much. It could have been burned up, or it may not have been here in the first place. We didn't find any proof at the accident in the desert.'

'It was the same for where Michelle saw the creature this morning, and the alley you and I were at last night.' He paused for a few seconds. 'How did the fire-fighter know to call you?'

'He'd heard about our part in what happened last night. I guess one of the police must have told him. Even though the army are trying to keep things quiet, they haven't been able to stop rumours from spreading.'

'Have the army offered any sort of cover story about why they're handling this instead of the fire-fighters and police?'

'Officially they're saying it's a perfect opportunity to train under real-world conditions, but all the firemen and police know the army is only here because the creature was, or at least that they think it might have been. We have, like, three house-fires a year in this town, and none of them are anywhere near this bad. It's a pretty bizarre coincidence for one to occur on the same night an unidentified animal appeared.'

Manny scanned the wreckage again, then looked back at Carla. 'There doesn't seem to be any more we can do here. Let's return to the campus and see if the guys examining Michelle's car have found anything useful.'

'You do that. There are a few other things I need to take care of.'

'Like what?' Manny asked.

'I'll let you know when I'm done.' She turned away.

'One more thing,' Manny said. 'I invited Grace to my house tonight so I can update her on whatever we've learned about the creature. In case I don't see you again before then, you should drop by too. Sometime around sundown.'

'I'll be there,' Carla assured him.

Without another word she started down the street to where she had parked the jeep, intent on fulfilling whatever mission she had on her mind, leaving Manny to wonder how exactly he was going to get back to the engineering workshop halfway across town.

Chapter 9

A heavy knock on the door pulled Manny out of his studies. He glanced at his watch. Five o'clock had come around faster than it seemed possible. Still, he had used the time constructively, digging into the mountain of homework that lay before him. He had even managed to forget about the creature – at least for a little while. He pulled himself up from the desk and arched his back in an attempt to remove some of the stiffness that he felt. He left his room and made his way to the lounge, already knowing who was outside.

He met Carla at the door, surprised to find her struggling under the weight of several large baking dishes. The late afternoon sun was edging closer to the horizon behind her, but the air was still hot.

'What's all this?' he asked, taking some of the pile from her.

'Call me crazy, but I have a feeling you probably haven't eaten much today.'

Manny held the door with his shoulder as she stepped inside. 'Too much on my mind,' he explained. 'Although I was thinking about ordering a pizza.'

They crossed the lounge room and placed the food on the kitchen table. 'Then I suppose it's a good thing I brought these along. I'm in the mood for home-cooking, and I don't think it will do you any harm either.' She looked him over critically, perhaps noticing a few bulges that hadn't been there until recently. 'When was the last time you ate something that wasn't deep-fried?'

Manny started to set the table and wouldn't meet her eyes.

'I thought as much. I'll have to speak with your mother.' Carla took a quick peek into the bedroom. 'Is she here tonight?'

'Not at the moment. One of the other nurses left town, so she's been taking a few extra shifts until a replacement can be found.'

Carla laughed quietly. 'At least that explains why you haven't had a decent meal lately.' She opened one of the dishes and started scooping food onto a plate.

'So,' Manny prompted, 'are you going to tell me what you've been doing all day? Besides cooking, I mean.'

'I've been thinking about the army's temporary base. It looks pretty permanent to me, which suggests the creature is going to be around for a while.'

'You really think so?'

'That's my guess. As far as I can tell, it came in a straight line – from the army base, to the accident site, and then here into Carlton. If it had kept moving in that line, Michelle wouldn't have seen it this morning because it would have already passed out of town. The fact that it hasn't suggests it's here to stay.'

'If that's the case, shouldn't someone else have seen it by now?'

'Not if it's hiding somewhere.'

'Any idea where that might be?'

'Most likely somewhere deserted. I think it would try to avoid humans. Maybe the industrial district. If we're lucky that's where it's set up house. Better there than in the residential area.'

Manny nodded thoughtfully. 'Makes sense. But how does that help us?'

'Well, we know the army aren't going to share any information, so if we want to learn about the creature we'll have to do it ourselves, and examining places it's been hours after it's already gone just isn't going to work. We need to study it directly. Which is why I've spent the day talking to anyone I thought might be willing to help us search for it. Since you were already planning to have Grace come over, I told the others to meet here as well.'

'How many should I expect?'

'Only a dozen or so. But don't worry about the house getting trashed. I've made sure everyone knows this is a serious situation, not a party. I told most of them to meet here at six to give us time to brainstorm. I did ask Cameron, Charlotte and Luke to stop by sooner. They're all pretty bright and I figured the six of us could bounce some ideas around before the rest arrive.' She checked her watch. 'What time did you tell Grace to stop by?'

'I said about sundown, but I'm not sure she'll show. She seemed eager to help this morning, but she may have changed her mind since then.'

'I think you're wrong about that,' Carla said, a little too casually.

Manny furrowed his brow. 'What's that supposed to mean?'

'Nothing,' Carla said innocently. 'I just think she may surprise you.'

Manny carefully scrutinised her, wondering for a moment if she'd hit her head during the day. She seemed to be acting more strangely than usual. He shook the idea out of his brain.

The sound of a car pulling up in front the house stopped any further discussion. Carla pushed the curtain aside and looked out the window.

'Who is it?' Manny asked.

'Charlotte and Cameron. They were checking the warehouses in the same part of town where we saw the creature last night.' She let the curtain fall shut and went back to her meal. Moments later the front door opened. Charlotte entered first with Cameron coming in a few seconds later.

'Anything?' Carla asked immediately.

In answer Charlotte shook her head. 'We were out there for an hour or more, but the area's so big, and we didn't leave the car. There must be dozens of deserted buildings which would make a perfect hiding spot.' She ran her fingers through her hair and wiped the sweat from her forehead. 'Do you have any cold water? It's frying out there.'

'In the fridge,' Manny told her.

She pulled two bottles free, handed one to Cameron, then sat down beside Manny. Cameron took a sip then set the bottle on the counter. He reached into his back pocket and pulled out a wad of paper. He spread it out on the table in front of Manny and the others. It was a map of the town and surrounding desert. He placed some of Carla's dishes around the edges to hold it down flat.

'What's this?' Manny asked.

'Carla's idea,' Cameron explained. 'We can write down all the places we know the creature has been. We've already marked where Michelle encountered it this morning, as well as the route you and Carla followed last night. If we do this for long enough we'll be able to see where the creature likes to hang out. Then we can advise people where the high risk areas are.'

Manny was thoughtful for a few seconds. 'I saw a map like this when I was being interviewed by Colonel Markham.'

'So did I,' Carla admitted. 'They quizzed me about the route we ran last night, so I knew they wanted to keep track of where it had been. That's what gave me the idea.'

'Have there been any other sightings?' Manny asked.

'Not exactly,' Charlotte said. 'Someone was killed early this morning on the edge of the industrial district. It happened in an alley, so no-one actually saw it occur, but it presents exactly like the woman in the desert. The police have released an official statement advising people to stay indoors where possible and to avoid unnecessary travel. They're still using the "unknown animal" story. I guess that's the best they could come up with.'

'Confining people to their houses isn't going to help if this thing really can pass through solid objects,' Manny said.

'How is that even possible?' Charlotte asked.

'I was talking to a zoology student earlier,' Carla put in. 'She had never heard of anything like it. Passing through solid objects and transparency aren't exactly common characteristics. Her best guess is that it's somehow able to alter its molecular density at will. That would explain how it can phase through things, but doesn't fall into the ground.'

'Did she have any idea of where it might have come from, or how it came to exist?'

'We tossed a few ideas around – alien, supernatural, genetic experiment gone wrong, as yet undiscovered life-form – but without more information all we can do is speculate.'

There was silence for a moment, and Manny realised they had already reached the end of everything they knew about the creature. 'I guess we can't brainstorm any more until we know more about it. And the only way we can do that is if we can somehow find it.'

'Do you want to leave right away?' Charlotte asked.

'I think that'll be best. You guys can stay here and strategize if you like, or if you're ready to go out again we can break into teams. That'll be safer than going out alone. Though we'll need at least one person to remain behind to meet up with anyone else who stops by.'

'I'll come with you,' Carla volunteered. She turned to the others. 'You two can stay here. After all, you've just come in from searching.'

'I guess that settles it,' Manny said. He stood up and crossed the lounge, followed closely by Carla.

He opened the front door and stepped back in surprise. Grace stood there with her hand up, just about to knock.

'Good afternoon,' Carla said. She turned to Manny. 'You should bring Grace up to date on what's happening. We can leave a little later.' She turned and headed for the kitchen to talk some more with Charlotte and Cameron.

Grace stood somewhat awkwardly in the doorway, as if waiting for Manny to invite her inside. Instead he stepped past her onto the porch and took a seat, motioning for her to do the same.

'Did you find the place okay?' Manny asked.

'Yeah, but that wasn't the biggest problem.' Off Manny's puzzled gaze she added, 'I've been trying to convince myself all afternoon that this is all some sort of elaborate prank you play on the new students. I probably would have succeeded if I hadn't seen the crash in the desert and if the army hadn't set up camp in town. You have to admit it does sound pretty unbelievable.'

She looked up as another car came to a stop in front the house. Manny's friend Luke climbed out, then reached in through the rear window and retrieved a cardboard box from the back seat. As he crossed the lawn, Manny and Grace were able to see a pair of binoculars, several charts and a torch sticking out the top of the carton. Luke nodded at the two in greeting and then entered the house.

'I didn't really expect this,' Grace said. 'You guys are pretty organised.'

'This is mostly Carla's idea. Since it looks like the creature is going to be around for a while, it needs to be taken seriously. The army aren't going to share information with us, so we'll have to work it out ourselves,' he explained. 'So far all we really know about it is that it's transparent and can pass through things.'

Manny stood up and took Grace's hand, helping her to her feet.

'Have you eaten this afternoon?' he asked.

'I had a little before I left my apartment.'

'Well, you should come in and get a feel for the place. If the situation goes on for a while, you'll probably be spending a lot of time here.' He opened the door and held it for her as she stepped inside. 'I'll give you the tour. This is the lounge, over there is the kitchen, and down the hall are the bedrooms and bathroom.' He stopped short. 'That's about it.'

'That doesn't seem like too much to remember.'

As they went to join the others at the table, Cameron came down the hall from the direction of Manny's bedroom, screwing the back onto a torch. He flicked the switch to ensure it was working properly. A loud bang immediately echoed through the room. Carla let out a surprised gasp.

'Sorry,' Cameron said. He bent over and poked at the flashlight, which now lay smoking on the floor. 'I have no idea why it did that. All I did was replace the batteries.'

Manny examined the smouldering remains. 'Is that my torch?' he asked.

'I guess so. It was in your bedroom.'

'That explains it. There's a short in it somewhere. It draws more power than it should. I've been meaning to throw it out.'

'You need to be more careful,' Charlotte said to Cameron. After hastily abandoning her position at the table thanks to the initial explosion, she now looked intent on reclaiming some of her lost dignity. She carefully inspected Cameron for burns. Like Manny, Charlotte was a medical student, so Cameron was in good hands.

'What happens now?' Grace asked Manny, getting back to more important matters.

'Carla and I were just about to take a drive around to see if we can find the creature. If you want you can come along, but since we don't know much about it yet, it might be best for you to stay here, especially since you don't know the streets very well. You can man the phone and help co-ordinate anybody who comes by. Aside from that there's not a lot to do, but it has the big plus of being safer than on the streets. I don't know if you heard or not, but someone else was killed today.'

Grace took a moment to consider her options. 'You make staying here sound like a good idea, but I've never been one to sit around. I think I'll come along. I'll learn the layout of the town better if I see it first-hand.'

'If you're sure...,' Manny said hesitantly.

'I am. And if something does go wrong, I'll have you to protect me.'

Manny didn't tell her that if something went wrong he wasn't even sure he could protect himself. He knew she understood the risks and hadn't made her decision lightly.

The world outside began to darken as the sun slipped below the horizon. Manny glanced through the window and saw a discarded soda can roll past on the footpath, pushed by a light breeze. Grace followed his gaze. The air had been warmer when she arrived a few minutes earlier, but since then it had cooled considerably.

'Do you think these will be okay?' she asked, indicating her clothes. She was wearing running shoes, a pair of jeans and a white long-sleeved blouse over a pale blue T-shirt. Slung over her shoulder was an old backpack. 'I also have a jacket in the car.'

'They look fine,' Manny said. 'What about your pack? Do you want to bring it along or leave it here?'

'I'll take it with me. I brought a few things from home that I thought might come in handy. I didn't realise you guys were this organised,' she said, repeating her earlier sentiment. She was referring to the now sizable pile of items on the kitchen table.

'What did you bring?' Manny asked.

'Just the basics.' She handed him her pack. 'A torch, some sandwiches, a bottle of water and a pair of walkie-talkies. I replaced the batteries this afternoon.'

'Good idea,' Manny said. 'I don't think we have any radios.' He paused for a second. 'How did you know we were going to be tracking the creature?'

'Carla called earlier to let me know. I spent the rest of the day trying to figure out what sort of equipment would come in handy. I thought radios might make it a bit easier to stay in touch with everyone.'

'Carla called you?' Manny asked, a little confused.

'Yeah. She wanted to make sure I planned on stopping by.'

Manny let the subject drop and instead flipped the walkie-talkie over and opened the back, checking the batteries. They were new, just as Grace had said. 'What's the range on these?' he asked.

'Pretty good. At least a few kilometres. Is that enough?'

Not bothering to answer her he called out, 'Charlotte.'

Immediately Charlotte hurried to his side. 'Ready to go?' she asked. She saw Grace standing beside him, but knew this wasn't the time for pleasantries.

'Yeah. Grace is going to come along with Carla and I.'

'The rest of us have been talking and we think we should all head out. The more of us there are the greater chance we have of spotting it.'

'Okay,' Manny said, quickly altering his plan. 'We'll split into groups of two. Grace can come with me into the residential area. Meanwhile you and Carla check the warehouses again. Luke and Cameron can search the centre of town.' He handed her one of Grace's walkie-talkies. 'We'll be able to keep in touch with these. I'll leave a note on the door for anyone else who shows up. If we can't find the creature in the next half hour or so, we'll meet back here to plan our next move.' He grabbed a pen, paper and tape from the side table and started to compose the note, while Charlotte went to inform everyone else what was happening.

Soon the group had assembled on the front lawn. The sun was well below the horizon by now, and night was firmly established. Lights shone from the windows of most of the houses along the street.

Manny held the door for Grace as she climbed into his jeep. He stood for a moment, watching as the other two vehicles left for their respective destinations, then he dropped Grace's backpack into the tray and took his place behind the wheel.

Chapter 10

They had been out for about half an hour without any sign of the creature when Manny decided it was time to return home. He pulled over to the side of the road and turned off the engine, then lifted the radio to his lips.

'Charlotte, are you there?'

'I'm here,' came a voice from the other end.

'Grace and I still haven't seen it. I think it's time we all go back to my place to see if we can come up with a better idea.'

'Sounds good. We'll turn around now.' There was a moment of silence before her voice came back on the line. 'What about Luke and Cameron? They don't have a radio.'

'Grace and I will go into the city centre and see if we can track them down. We'll meet you at my house in a few minutes.'

'Okay, we'll see you there.'

Manny slipped the radio onto his belt, then restarted the car and pulled into the street. Houses blurred past as they proceeded deeper into the city. Puddles of water from the storm the night before still sat in the drains on the edge of the road, as well as a few in the street itself, forcing Manny to take extra care. He mostly kept his eyes on the road, leaving Grace to look for Luke and Cameron.

'Manny, wait,' Grace suddenly commanded.

'What is it?' Manny asked, bringing the car to an abrupt halt.

'There are some people back there,' she said, pointing to a side road they had passed.

Looking over his shoulder, Manny was just able to see the front of the car in question.

'Is it Cameron and Luke?' he asked.

'I think so,' Grace said. 'I didn't really get a good look.'

Manny undid his seatbelt, climbed from the jeep and walked back towards the other vehicle.

After a quick glance of her own, which satisfied her there was no danger, Grace followed.

As she drew closer she saw Luke and Cameron standing by the boot of the car, staring intently in the opposite direction. They were parked across the road from a toyshop. A string of coloured lights flickered in the window, obviously connected to an outlet somewhere in the store.

'What's up?' Manny asked as he arrived beside the car.

The two young men jumped in surprise. As they turned and saw Manny, they visibly relaxed.

'I heard something down the street,' Cameron answered. 'I thought it might be the creature.'

'Was it?'

'Don't know. We couldn't see anything.'

'How long ago did you hear it?' Manny asked.

'Only a minute or so,' Cameron replied. 'It probably wasn't the creature. Maybe just a cat or something.'

The three guys stared off into the darkness trying to discern what had caused the sound, while Grace kept watch to ensure the creature didn't appear from another direction.

Finally deciding there was nothing to worry about, Manny got back to the reason they were there.

'I've just been on the radio to Charlotte. We agree it's time to return to my place so we can come up with another plan.'

'That sounds like a good idea,' Cameron said, moving towards the passenger side door of the car. Before he could get in, he turned abruptly. 'You should also know, we're not the only ones trying to find the creature.'

'The army?' Manny asked.

'They're around, but I'm actually talking about people like us. A few minutes ago we stopped a car of other college students to try to talk them out of looking for it but they wouldn't listen. We figured if they were going to be here anyway, they may as well be doing something useful, so we sent them back to your place to be involved in the next sweep.'

'To be honest, I'm surprised there aren't more people doing the same thing.'

'Oh, there are,' Luke cut in. 'That was the car we stopped. But there have been about six others we've seen.'

Manny was taken aback. 'Isn't anyone listening to the police's instructions not to travel unnecessarily?'

'I guess not, but it doesn't really matter. The police don't have the manpower to enforce it, and the soldiers are all hanging out closer to the city centre. Maybe that's where they think the creature is most likely to show. We've been trying to stay out of their way.'

As the other three continued to talk, Grace looked across the road to the toyshop. Knowing it was closed for the night, but hoping the lights in the windows were an indication it was still open for business, she hurried over. Manny came up behind her as she was trying the door. It was locked.

'What is it?' he asked.

'I was hoping there would be some more walkie-talkies in there,' she explained. 'I doubt we'll be able to convince everyone to remain inside, especially since we have no intention of doing it ourselves, but if we distribute some radios, at least we'll all be able to stay in contact with each other.'

'Good thinking.' He turned his attention to Luke. 'See if you can track down anyone else who is out here on the streets. Tell them to gather at my house. I'll try to find a few extra radios and then meet you back there.'

Luke looked a little perturbed at being delegated as errand boy, but conceded that the idea was sound. 'Okay, I'll see you there.'

He climbed into his car and turned the key. The engine roared to life. Then came another noise. Something at the end of the street clattered to the ground. Though Grace heard it too, it didn't really register with her. She only became concerned when she saw Manny freeze.

'Wait,' Manny called to Luke.

Luke stopped the engine.

'No,' Manny warned, 'keep it running.' Doing as he was asked, Luke restarted the car.

'Is that the creature?' Grace asked.

Manny stared down the street. 'I don't know. I'll check it out. Wait here and be ready. We may need to get out of here fast.' He started jogging towards the source of the noise. He knew it was foolhardy, but he had to find out if their assumptions about the creature were accurate. Though Michelle had vouched it was mostly invisible and able to pass through solid matter, he needed to confirm it for himself.

Watching Manny disappear into the darkness made Grace feel decidedly uneasy. As strange as it sounded, she had come to trust him over the course of the last two days, and didn't want anything to happen to him. She knew if the town had any hope of ridding itself of the creature, it would be with Manny's help. Plus, she felt safer when he was by her side.

She followed him slowly, glancing from side to side, expecting a black fog to come out of every shadow. At the edge of the toyshop she stepped onto the road and immediately felt her shoe slide into a puddle left by the previous evening's rain. Startled by the coolness of the water, she stumbled, falling to her hands and knees. But in that moment of confusion, she saw everything clearly; the cracked and broken pavement of the sidewalk, the streetlights, the puddles along the road and something much worse. Coming out of an alley on the other side of the toyshop was the creature. She opened her mouth to call out, to warn Cameron and Luke of the danger, but before she could find the words, they too saw it lumber out of the darkness.

It didn't look like the black fog she had been expecting. It was almost completely transparent, aside from the occasional spark that seemed to come from inside of it. By the way it moved Grace knew it wasn't just an entity – it was an animal. It was as high as the nearby car and about half as long. There was a strange protrusion at the front of the bubble and Grace realised she was looking at the creature's head.

For the moment it was focused solely on Luke's car, giving Grace a few free seconds to plan her next move. Luke, who had climbed out of the car as Manny started down the road, was now edging along the footpath on the far side of the street, obviously preparing to assist her if the need arose. Cameron stood nearby, torn between the desire to flee and fear that the creature would chase him if he did.

Luke moved closer, at the same time nodding towards the car. Grace understood what he was trying to say. They needed to escape before the creature turned its attention to them.

Suddenly her eyes widened in fear. The creature was no longer looking at the vehicle, but instead was focused entirely on Luke. Grace frantically gestured for him to freeze, but it was already too late. The creature darted towards him. A streetlight stood between the two, but it was no obstacle. The creature stepped through the pole as though it wasn't there. The light up top flickered and died. A strange prickling sensation passed from Grace's feet to the top of her head. The hairs on the back of her neck seemed to stand up. As the creature stepped out of the pole, the streetlight came back on.

Luke saw the creature coming in his direction and started to flee. Unfortunately, as he turned, he ran straight into a street sign.

Cameron immediately went to his friend's aid, catching Luke as he stumbled around in pain, then pulling him back towards the car.

All this activity seemed to momentarily confuse the creature. It stopped moving, but Grace knew it was only a matter of time before it regained its senses and attacked. Already she could see its focus shifting back to where Cameron was struggling to get Luke into the car.

His efforts were admirable, but now both of them stood in the creature's path. Unless something happened to give Cameron the time to rescue his friend, they were doomed. And since Manny was too far away to be any help at all, Grace knew it was up to her.

She looked towards the streetlight, at the same time remembering the faint sparks flickering inside the creature and the way it had drained the batteries of three different cars. There was a connection there and she suddenly knew what it was.

Quickly Grace returned to the front of the toyshop and rammed her elbow through the window. It shattered immediately and shards of glass rained down around her. The creature turned at the distraction, but she wasn't done yet. She grabbed the string of flashing lights. They were secured to the windowsill with tape but she managed to pull them free. With all the speed she could muster, Grace dragged the lights through the opening and dropped the bundle into a puddle on the edge of the street. Sparks flew as she shielded her eyes.

The creature started towards the disturbance. Grace turned on her heels and ran, yelling back to Cameron, 'Get in the car and go.'

Her footsteps thudded on the pavement at a frantic pace. She saw Manny ahead of her, jogging back to see what was going on.

Without bothering to explain the situation she called to him, 'Run.'

That one word was enough to tell him all he needed to know.

She reached Manny in an instant, then passed him by. A moment later the sound of his footsteps told Grace he was sprinting as well.

All too soon they reached the end of the street. They had been running towards the T in a T-road and Grace knew if she chose the wrong direction it could get them both killed.

'Which way?' she yelled to Manny, who was still a few steps behind.

'Through the garden,' he called back.

Trusting him completely she pushed herself harder, jumping over the fence, barely slowing as she made heavy contact with the earth on the other side. She heard Manny land less than a second after herself. She glanced back, relieved to see he was still on his feet.

He drew level with her as they dodged past the house. Then, after being in the yard for less than five seconds, they exited over the back fence. They ran through the next yard, thankful there were no other obstacles to slow them down. Manny overtook as they made it back onto the road. Grace could barely believe it when he headed straight for a two metre high wooden paling fence.

She was about to give in to fatigue when she saw him step onto a garbage can beside the fence and use it to jump over. As she followed suit she heard a splash from inside the yard. A moment after she leaped she found herself neck-deep in a swimming pool. Ignoring the steady ache she felt all over, Grace half-swam, half-dragged herself to the far side of the pool. She pulled herself up next to Manny, who had already made it through the water. She took a deep breath and prepared to set off again. As she started to move she felt Manny grab her.

He held his finger to his lips and whispered, 'I think we lost it.'

Grace was shocked to realise he was right. She had been so busy running that she had stopped focusing on the creature. She wondered briefly how far it had chased them, or if it had chased them at all.

Between ragged breaths Manny asked her, 'Where are the others?'

'I don't know,' she answered. 'I was already running when I told Cameron to get out of there. I heard the car start moving, but that's all I know for sure.' Completely worn out, Grace felt herself sliding down the wall at her back. A moment later Manny collapsed beside her. 'Was the creature even following us?' she asked.

'It chased us down the road, but after we went through the first yard I lost track of it.' He reached down to his belt for the radio Grace had given him. Even at a glance he could see it was beyond repair. He held it up as the last of the water from the pool drained out of it.

'You'll have to pay for that,' Grace joked.

He let out a small chuckle.

'It wasn't that funny.'

'It's not that.'

'Then what?' she asked.

'We've been trying to make sure everyone else has a radio, but now we don't have one.'

They lapsed into an easy silence for a few minutes, before Grace asked, 'What do we do now?'

'We'd better rest a little longer, just in case we run into it again. Then we'll have to find somewhere safe. I think my house is a bit too far away to manage at the moment, especially without a car, and I don't want to go back to the jeep in case the creature is still in the area. I suppose we can try the supermarket. It's open pretty late. We may be able to find someone there who will give us a ride.'

They waited a few minutes more, gathering their strength, then made their way past the pool and back towards the street. Manny stopped at the gate and peeked out. Though there was no indication the creature was nearby, he wanted to be extra careful. When he was satisfied it was safe, the two of them left the yard and started for the supermarket.

Chapter 11

Fifteen minutes after receiving the call from Manny telling them he was going to track down Cameron and Luke in the city centre, Carla and Charlotte were still waiting anxiously in Manny's kitchen for the others to return.

Through the open doorway they could hear the quiet discussions of the new arrivals who had gathered in the backyard. Most were the people Carla had recruited during the day, but there were also some from a car Cameron and Luke had stopped in the city centre, as well as a few more who had somehow heard about what was happening and decided to volunteer.

The sound of a car pulling up in front of the house immediately caught Carla's attention. Together with Charlotte, she abandoned her position at the kitchen table and headed for the front door, ready to greet Manny and the others as they arrived back. They were halfway across the lounge room when Cameron burst in with Luke leaning heavily on his shoulder. The two girls stopped in surprise.

'It's not what it looks like,' Cameron explained. 'We were running from the creature and he hit his head.'

The shock passed quickly and Carla helped Cameron lay Luke on the couch. She carefully scrutinised his stricken form. Especially obvious was a large bruise in the centre of his forehead. 'It might be a good idea to get him to hospital.'

'It's only a bump,' Luke said.

Carla didn't seem convinced. 'It's a head wound. Manny says you should always be careful with them. And I can see some blood there.' She turned to Charlotte. 'See if you can find a first aid kit. There should be one in the bathroom cabinet. If not, try under the sink in the kitchen.'

Charlotte nodded wordlessly and disappeared down the hall in the direction of the bathroom.

Luke brushed away her concern. 'It's fine. Anyway, the creature's still out there somewhere. That's what we should be thinking about.'

His words reminded Carla of her primary concern. 'Did you guys see Manny?'

'Yeah. We were talking to him just before we were attacked,' Luke said.

Carla was suddenly scared. 'Where is he now?'

'Manny and Grace ran off towards the city centre,' Cameron said quickly.

Carla shook her head, silently cursing herself for convincing the others that tracking the creature was a good idea. She had been organising people all day, almost like a game. But now, with Manny out somewhere in the night, things had started to feel very real.

Her thoughts were interrupted as Charlotte arrived back from the bathroom carrying the first aid kit. Carla moved out of the way to allow Charlotte access to Luke. Charlotte shared several classes with Manny, and Carla knew she was more than competent. While Charlotte cleaned the wound on Luke's head, Carla and Cameron moved into the kitchen.

'What happened out there?' Carla asked.

'Luke and I were just about to head back when we heard something up the street. Before we could investigate, Manny and Grace arrived. I guess they must have seen us as they were driving past. There was another noise and Manny went to check it out. That's when the creature came out of an alley right near us. It started chasing Luke, which is when he hit the sign. It probably would have killed him like the others, except Grace distracted it. It took off after her, and I got Luke into the car. I started after Grace and Manny, hoping I could get ahead and pick them up, but by the time I caught them, they were already in the backyards. I considered trying to meet them on the next street, but I decided I'd better get Luke back here as soon as possible. He seems better now, but after I got him in the car he passed out. Also, the creature started chasing us again, and I didn't want to lead it to Manny and Grace.'

Charlotte entered the kitchen as Cameron finished talking.

'How's Luke doing?' Carla asked.

'He seems fine. I don't think there's a concussion, but it's probably a good idea to take him to the hospital in the morning. That's the only way to be completely sure he's okay. The blood was from a small cut, so he won't need stitches or anything.'

'At least that's one thing off my mind.'

Charlotte saw Carla's eyes fall and did what she could to console her. 'Manny knows how to handle himself. He's bound to be back any minute now.'

'I think I'll give him a call, just to make sure,' Carla said. She pulled a walkie-talkie from her pocket and put it to her lips. 'Manny, can you hear me?' She waited a few seconds for a reply, then asked again, 'Manny, are you there?' When she failed to receive an answer on her second attempt she checked that the radio was on the right channel. It was.

Carla felt a stab of panic. 'Why won't he respond?' Before the others could reply, she answered her own question. 'Something must have happened to him.'

'He probably just turned his radio off to ensure the creature wouldn't hear it,' Cameron said.

His words made sense but Carla still moved towards the door.

'You're not thinking of going out there alone, are you?' Charlotte asked, already knowing the answer. She grabbed Carla by the arm. 'That could be suicide.'

'Manny wouldn't leave me out there. I have to do the same for him.' Carla struggled against Charlotte's grip. Charlotte released her and went to pick up a torch from the kitchen table. Carla was already halfway out the door.

'Wait,' Charlotte called.

Carla looked back to see Charlotte striding across the floor.

'I'm not asking you to come.'

'If you're serious about this then you're going to need someone to watch your back.'

'Guys, this isn't a good idea,' Cameron broke in. 'You have no idea where Manny and Grace are. The best thing we can do is wait here until he contacts us. He wouldn't want either of you to put yourself at risk for nothing.'

'I'm not leaving Manny out there alone.'

'He's not alone,' Cameron said. 'He has Grace with him.'

'You know what I mean,' Carla cut back.

'Grace is a lot more resourceful than you give her credit for. She saved Luke and me from almost certain death. Neither of them is stupid. Either they'll come straight back here as soon as possible, or they'll call and let us know what they're doing.'

'And if they don't?'

'I know a few people who live near the centre of town. I'll give them a call and ask them to be on the lookout for Manny and Grace.'

Though Carla still wanted desperately to leave, she could see the sense behind Cameron's idea. 'I guess you're right,' she said. She turned around and headed for the back door.

'Now what are you up to?' Charlotte asked.

'I'm going to keep watch from on the roof.' Before the other two could protest, Carla stepped outside. She grabbed a ladder from under the porch, leaned it against the house and started to climb.

The roof of the house wasn't steep. In fact, Manny and Carla would often hang out there. Usually they would just sit and talk, but tonight Carla had another agenda. Standing on the roof she was high enough above the ground to see over the neighbouring houses, and sitting atop the chimney gave her a good view of the nearby blocks. From this position she was sure to see Manny as he arrived back.

For a moment she let her gaze linger over the people gathered in the backyard. The mood was cheerful, and Carla realised none of them had any idea of the danger they were putting themselves in.

Chapter 12

Manny and Grace arrived at the supermarket in silence. The front doors opened automatically as they approached. Together they entered the mall, eager to leave the darkness and the cold behind them.

The first shop they came to was a fast food outlet. The smell of roasting meat and warm coffee reminded Manny of just how hungry he was. He decided to forget about finding a lift until they had both eaten something. He held the door for Grace as they entered the restaurant.

Considering there was a terrifying creature roaming the night, Manny had expected the store to be deserted. Instead it was somewhat crowded. He guessed that being around other people and bright lights made everyone feel safer than they would have if they were in their own home.

'Find a table. I'll get us something to eat,' Manny instructed Grace. She nodded as he approached the front counter.

'How can I help you?' the cashier asked.

'Two burgers would be good,' he said, then added, 'and two coffees.' Their clothes had mostly dried as they travelled through the streets, but they were both still cold.

'No problem. Someone will be over with your order shortly.'

Manny dropped some money on the counter. 'Is there any place around here that sells walkie-talkies?'

'If you're lucky they haven't closed the electronics shop for the night. It's a few doors down.'

Manny nodded. 'Thanks. Keep the change.' He walked over to where Grace was sitting, in a booth by the store entrance. She was staring intently through the windows and out into the parking lot.

'I don't think you need to worry,' he said.

Grace turned at the interruption. 'I'm not worried, but I am trying to be prepared. Someone needs to be keeping watch.'

'Someone is,' Manny said, nodding towards a group of college students standing outside on the corner. 'I also saw some people up on the roof as we came in.' He glanced towards the door.

'Somewhere you'd rather be?' Grace inquired.

'There's a shop nearby that sells walkie-talkies. I'm going to see if it's still open. I'll be back in a minute.'

Grace nodded, then returned her gaze to the parking lot.

As Manny left the restaurant, he noticed a bank of payphones along the wall. He realised the others back at his house would have no idea what had happened to him and Grace.

He picked up a handset and inserted a few coins into the side of the phone, then dialled his own number.

Charlotte picked up on the first ring. 'Manny?' she asked quickly.

'That's right. What's going on?'

She seemed to breathe a sigh of relief. 'I was worried about you. Luke and Cameron arrived back and filled us in on what happened. How are you and Grace?'

'We're both fine. After we lost the creature I didn't want to return to the jeep in case it was still in the area, and since it was too far for us to make it home without a car, we came to the mall instead.' He paused briefly, then continued, 'If I hadn't run off we all would have arrived back there together. I shouldn't have deserted them like that.'

'As I understand it, you left to investigate what you thought was the creature. That was brave.'

'It was foolish. But I needed to see it again, to know if what I thought I saw the other night was accurate.'

'Was it?'

Manny laughed humourlessly. 'I don't know. It was chasing Grace, and I started running too, so I didn't get a good look. But it's definitely transparent. Almost invisible.'

'Cameron and Luke said the same thing. They also told me about your idea to track down more walkie-talkies, so I called some people who I thought might be able to help. Now we have plenty, so you won't need to worry about finding any more.' There was silence for a moment, then Charlotte added, 'I should probably get off the phone now.'

'Okay.'

'Are you planning on coming back here tonight?' Charlotte asked, almost as an afterthought.

'Yeah. Grace and I are having something to eat at the moment, but afterwards I'll try to catch a lift with someone.'

'Let me know if you can't. I can send one of the guys from here to pick you up.'

'No problem.'

'I guess I'll see you in a few minutes,' Charlotte said, hanging up the phone.

Manny replaced the receiver and returned to Grace. Two trays, each with a coffee and a burger, sat on the table in front of her.

Noticing that he was empty-handed, Grace asked, 'Was the electronics shop closed?'

'No. I called Charlotte and she said they had already tracked down some more radios, so I decided not to worry about it.'

He took the seat across from Grace and started on his burger. For several minutes the two ate in silence. Though neither mentioned it, the short, frantic run through the streets had taken its toll on them both.

They finished eating and set the trays aside.

'I think we need to have a serious talk about the creature,' Manny said. 'So far you're one of the few people who's seen it up close. Anything you noticed could be a big help to us. You can start by telling me what happened after I went down the street.'

Grace took a moment to get everything straight in her head, then began to explain.

'You'd only been gone for about half a minute when the creature came out of the alleyway beside the toyshop. It was transparent, like you said, but inside of it I could see what looked like sparks. At first it seemed more interested in the car than us, but then it started after Luke, and when he tried to escape he hit his head on a street sign. As it went for him it passed through a streetlight, making the light go out. At the same time I felt this weird prickling sensation. That's what gave me the idea to use the string of lights from the toyshop to distract it.'

'What do you mean?' Manny broke in.

'The light went out was because the creature drained all its power. The prickling sensation I felt was static electricity. I figure the creature was full and was releasing the excess energy. Don't you see? The creature feeds on electricity because that's what it's made of.'

'That's why it was originally going for the car. The key was on and the battery would have been giving off energy,' Manny said, finally understanding.

'Right,' Grace agreed. 'But after we started moving around, I guess it got confused and that's why it began chasing us.'

Once more they lapsed into companionable silence, both staring through the front windows of the store and into the parking lot.

Suddenly there was movement in the group of college students gathered on the corner.

'It's coming down the street. Everybody get inside,' someone shouted.

Manny jumped out of the booth then helped Grace to her feet. Together they left the fast food store. Everyone who had been outside was quickly moving indoors. Manny grabbed the arm of a young man who was rushing past.

'Where is it?' Manny asked.

The guy pointed down the street. 'It's coming here, I know it is.'

Though it was still half a block away, Manny knew the young man's assessment of the situation had been accurate. The creature was headed for the shopping centre, the largest source of electricity in the area. It gelled perfectly with what Grace had said.

'Will the doors keep it out?' Grace asked. 'Is there any way to lock them?'

'They're automatic,' the young man answered. 'Only the centre manager can shut them off, and I haven't seen him tonight.'

'There are fire-escapes at the rear of the mall. If we can get everyone up on top of the building, they should be safe,' Manny said.

'There's no need to go outside. At the back of Food Mart there's a set of stairs that leads to the roof.' Food Mart was both the largest shop in the complex, and also the main grocery store in Carlton.

'Are you sure?' Manny asked.

'Yeah. I've worked here for two years.'

'Okay. Get everybody up on the roof,' Manny instructed.

The young man ran over to the last of the people coming in from the outside and told them the plan. As they ran off, Manny surveyed the doorway. Grace remained beside him, but clearly wanted to be elsewhere.

'We need to stop it getting inside,' Manny said.

Grace scanned the area. Several wheeled planter boxes sat nearby.

'Here,' she said. 'We can use these. They won't stop it but they may slow it down.'

The two of them quickly pushed six of the boxes in front of the doors.

With their job done, Grace headed deeper into the complex. Manny hung back for a moment, continuing to stare through the doors and out into the night. The creature was now close enough to be fully illuminated by the lights of the parking lot. It looked exactly as he thought, almost completely transparent, and inside of it he could see the sparks Grace had described. He watched for a few more seconds and then turned to follow Grace.

She was waiting for him at the entrance to Food Mart. Together they walked down an aisle to the back of the store, pushed through a set of plastic doors, then followed the signs that said "Roof Access" until they reached the stairs.

By the time they arrived on top of the building, most of the others had already fanned out around the edges in order to determine the creature's current position.

Manny approached the largest group.

'Where is it?' he asked.

'We can't see it. Either it's inside, or it's already left the area. My guess would be the former.'

'Did everyone make it up here?'

'A lot of people did, but a few ran off in other directions.'

'Is there somewhere safe nearby they could go?'

'Maybe. Most of the buildings around here have access to the roofs. Unless they decided to just keep running.'

But even as they spoke, some unfortunate soul decided they really were safer at the mall, with its thick walls and high roof. It was a young man, probably a college student, though Manny didn't recognise him. He was treading carefully, looking both ways, obviously trying to figure out if the creature was still in the area, not realising it was already inside.

'Hey,' Manny called, but the young man had disappeared into the complex. Manny started for the stairs.

Grace stopped him before he could leave the safety of the roof. 'What do you think you're doing?'

'Someone just entered the mall. He's not going to be safe until he's up here with the rest of us.'

'The creature's down there.'

Manny nodded grimly. 'I know. But it's a big mall. It could be anywhere.'

'Or it could be waiting for you at the bottom of the stairs. For all you know it was following us. First the desert, then the toyshop, and now here. It's a pretty big coincidence that it's been at all these places at the same time as us.'

'That doesn't change anything.'

Grace sighed and stood aside. 'I'll watch your back.'

Manny shook his head. 'No. You stay here. I won't be long.'

He approached the door that led inside, all the while feeling Grace's eyes on him.

Chapter 13

After descending the stairs and checking that the creature was nowhere nearby, Manny weaved his way through various corridors, doorways and aisles until he once again found himself at the entrance to Food Mart.

In front of him were three options. Straight ahead towards the fast food outlet where he and Grace had first arrived at the mall, or left or right to one of the other doors. He chose left, since that was where the young man had entered the complex.

As Manny walked, carefully scanning from side to side, he couldn't help but notice how much larger the mall seemed now that there was no-one else around. And that wasn't the only difference. Despite the cheerful music coming through the mall's speakers, and the brightly-lit, almost festive, displays at the front of each store, the building seemed so much more foreboding than it had been only minutes before.

His heart pounded in his chest as if he had run a marathon, even though he'd been walking more slowly and cautiously than ever before.

He reached the main entrance with no sign of the young man. On the plus side, he hadn't run into the creature either. He briefly wondered if it could have left the area as he made his way down from the roof.

As he looked out over the parking lot, a noise from behind made him turn. He nearly froze in shock. The young man he had been looking for was standing a few metres away at the front of a clothing store. Manny guessed he must have come out from inside.

'Where did everyone go?' the stranger asked.

'They're on top of the building. We think the creature is in the mall somewhere, and the roof seemed like the safest place to be.' He paused, not wanting to ask his next question, but knowing he had no choice. 'Is anyone else around?'

'I saw a few people, but they were all going the other way.'

'And you thought it would be worthwhile to investigate what they were running from?'

'It seemed like a good idea at the time.'

Manny could appreciate that. It was the same thought which had sent him onto the streets earlier in the night. Since then he had drastically reconsidered the intelligence behind such a notion. But he couldn't very well run away while there were people in danger.

He took one last look around and then turned to the young man. 'We should go up on the roof,' he said. 'It's not safe down here.'

Suddenly, some movement at the corner of his eye caught Manny's attention. Before he could cry out, the creature darted from a nearby shop and passed through the young man as though he wasn't there. He fell to the floor.

Though the creature was made of energy, Manny knew the young man hadn't been electrocuted. Every electrical impulse in his body had been instantly absorbed, causing immediate death. It was the same for the woman in the desert. Manny took a measure of comfort in the fact that neither had felt any pain.

But now he had bigger problems. The creature was standing only a few metres in front of him, in the middle of the corridor, blocking the shortest route to the safety of the roof. The only other way up to the top of the building was a fire-escape on the far side of the shopping centre. He wasn't sure he could outrun the creature again, but he didn't have any other option. He took several slow steps backward, out the main doors of the complex, hoping that the creature wouldn't notice him. But of course he wasn't that lucky. As he moved, the creature began to stare intently at him.

Manny froze, praying it would lose interest and go back to whatever it had been doing before he interrupted it. Instead it began to cautiously approach him. Manny came to possibly the most important decision of his life. His brain couldn't get him out of this predicament. He would have to rely on his legs.

He turned and bolted. His course carried him out into the parking lot and between several parked cars. He hoped navigating the gauntlet would at least slow the creature down. He didn't risk a look back to see if his gamble had been successful. Deep down he knew it hadn't. He could still hear the creature close behind. With stunning certainty he realised he had no chance of making it around to the far side of the mall and up onto the roof.

He abruptly altered his course, running down an alleyway and up a small set of stairs to a roller-door that led to the Food Mart stockrooms. If the door was open he could make his way back into the mall and get up onto the roof that way.

He glanced back in time to see the creature pass the alley, but he knew it would quickly realise its mistake. He reached for the door and tried to heave it upwards, but it stayed firmly in place. It was secured from the inside. He could feel the lock starting to give, but he didn't have the strength to push it all the way. There was a noise behind him and Manny knew the creature had entered the alley. He put all of his strength into one last attempt.

Suddenly he felt a presence beside him and another pressure on the roller-door. The door jerked upwards. Manny glanced sideways and almost stopped in shock. There beside him was Grace, having clambered down the roofs in order to come to his aid. She grabbed his shirt and yanked him into the building. When they were both safely inside she slammed the roller-door down. As Manny's eyes adjusted to the darkness, he saw they were in a vacant storeroom. Grace stood in front of him, scanning the room for an exit.

'What are you doing here?' Manny asked.

Grace didn't bother to answer. Instead she took him by the hand and dragged him to the door. 'We need to go. When the creature chased you in the parking lot it went straight through a seat and a railing. Though for some reason it went over the cars. If it wants in, I don't think there's any way to stop it.'

Outside the storeroom, Manny found himself in a larger loading bay with several corridors leading off in varying directions.

Driven by some internal guidance system, Grace quickly led Manny through the darkened hallways and back to the stairs they had used a few minutes earlier. Before she could ascend, she stopped. Now that the immediate danger was over, she had to ask.

'Did you find the guy you were looking for?'

'I did. The creature killed him. When we can get to a phone I'll call the police and army and let them know.'

They started up the stairs.

On top of the building, Manny quickly explained to everyone what had happened downstairs. By now he was desperate to get back home, not only so he would feel more at ease, but also so he could update Carla on all the new information they had. He asked around, but after hearing that the creature had killed someone, no-one was willing to leave the safety of the roof.

Disappointed, he returned to Grace. She was standing at the rear of the mall, staring thoughtfully into the darkness.

'What's the plan?' she asked.

'There's nothing more we can accomplish here. We should go back to my place and tell the others what we know.'

'How are we going to manage that?'

'The creature is probably still out there, but if we wait a few minutes, it should leave the area. In an alley on the next block there's a fire-escape that leads to the roof. From there we should be able to make it most of the way back to the jeep without setting foot on the ground.'

'Sounds good.'

As Grace went to turn away, Manny reached out a hand to stop her. 'Thanks for the help back there,' he said.

Grace shrugged. 'You would have done the same for me.'

Chapter 14

The pair arrived back at Manny's place half an hour later. Several more cars now sat on the lawn as well as on the street in front of his house, forcing Manny to park his jeep further down the block.

As they entered through the front door they found Charlotte sitting at the kitchen table with several college students. Yet more waited in the lounge room, pouring over maps of the town or sorting through piles of radios, torches and other equipment that might prove useful.

'You finally made it,' Charlotte said, abandoning the group at the table and hurrying over to Grace and Manny. 'I was starting to get worried. I thought you were going to come straight back here when you were done eating.'

'That was the plan, but things got a little complicated when the creature showed up,' Grace informed her.

Charlotte was instantly alarmed. 'Do you think it was following you?'

Manny shook his head. 'I doubt it. I think we were just in the wrong place at the wrong time.'

He looked around the room. There were at least a dozen college students in his house, most of them strangers, though that didn't fully account for all the cars out front. He guessed there must be more outside.

'How many people are here?' he asked.

'About twenty all up. Half in here and the rest in the backyard or up on the roof.'

'Are we expecting any others?'

'I don't think so, but we have set this place up as a sort-of home base, so you never know. There's been a steady stream of people dropping by over the past hour or so. I guess word is spreading about what we're doing. You should have seen it earlier; there were at least twice as many people here. We gave everyone radios and sent them out looking for the creature. We decided it was a bit risky to actually be walking the streets, so most of them are keeping watch from inside houses or up on the roofs.'

'Have they had any luck?' Manny asked.

'No. As far as I can tell, you and Grace and the others at the mall were the last to see it.' Charlotte looked towards the back door. 'I should let Carla know you've returned. She's been worried about you.'

'I'll go talk to her,' Manny offered.

'Then I guess I'll check on Luke again,' Charlotte said. She started for the guest bedroom but turned back when she reached the door.

'Have you two been swimming?' she asked. 'Your clothes are dry, but your hair looks kind of...,' she patted her head as if searching for the right word, '...flat.'

Manny and Grace shrugged.

Charlotte stared at them a moment longer then left the room.

Though it had been Manny's intention to find Carla straight away, he decided his first priority should be to contact the police and explain everything that had happened at the mall. The officer on the other end of the line assured him that the army would receive all the necessary information.

As soon as the call was complete, Manny went looking for Carla.

He found her sitting on a bench on the back veranda. In the far corner of the garden, several college students were involved in a heated debate about the creature. Other people were just lying there, looking up at the stars, but they were far enough away that Manny and Carla could talk in total privacy.

'What took you so long?' Carla asked, doing a good job of covering her concern.

'The creature arrived while we were at the mall. It killed someone and then chased me. If it hadn't been for Grace it would have killed me too. She's the most fearless person I've ever encountered.'

He thought Carla would be pleased, but instead he saw her face fall.

'What's the matter?' he asked.

'You've only known her for a day and you already trust her completely.'

'So this is about Grace?'

'I just think you need to be careful.'

'She saved my life at the supermarket. The creature had me cornered in an alleyway. The only reason I was able to escape was because Grace risked her life to help me. If she hadn't done that I would have been finished. As far as I'm concerned that's a good enough reason to trust her.'

Carla turned away, ashamed of the feelings she was having. Manny realised what was actually going on. 'This isn't just about Grace; it's about me and Grace.'

'I just worry sometimes,' Carla admitted.

'How long have we been friends?'

'All our lives.'

'And you seriously think I'm going to abandon you for a girl I've only known one day.'

'I've seen the way you look at her. You can't tell me that she's just another girl.'

'I admit she's nice to have around. But that's the extent of it. I don't have the time to date, and even if I did, there are bigger things to worry about.'

'So you've thought about it?'

'It crossed my mind. But that's all.'

'She's a nice girl, Manny.'

Suddenly he was confused. 'You want me to like her, but you don't want me to. Is that what you're saying?'

'I want you to like her, but I don't want you to forget about me.'

'I'm not going to forget about you. No-one could make that happen.' Another thought struck him. 'You were acting strangely yesterday, before we went to the airport, when I told you Grace was coming along. I didn't realise it at the time, but you were talking her up to me. Were you trying to see if I was interested in her?'

Carla nodded.

'Why?'

'I'd met her a few days earlier and thought she'd be perfect for you. I wanted to know if you felt the same way. If you did, I was planning to set the two of you up together.'

'Why would you do that if you were so worried about me forgetting you?'

'I want you to be happy.'

'I am happy.'

'I know,' Carla said, 'but sometimes I worry that you aren't.'

'It doesn't really matter. She's not interested in me in that way. I mean, on the second day I knew her I almost got her killed.'

Carla laughed softly. 'I think she's interested. I've seen her watching you the same way you watch her. She's probably waiting for you to make the first move.'

'Yeah, I can just picture it, "Hey Grace, want to spend the night with me chasing a monster around town?" That's not going to be the best pick-up line she's ever heard.'

'True, but it will be the most original,' Carla said.

'Do you mind if I get through the next few days first? A lot is going on, and I can't let myself get distracted.'

'Okay, but don't wait too long. A girl that "fearless" isn't going to wait around forever. There are plenty of guys out there who are already very interested.'

Manny chuckled a little. 'She's smart too.'

'How do you mean?'

'She realised the creature is an electrically-based life-form,' Manny said.

'That's ridiculous. Electricity can't just come alive.'

'But electricity exists within people. If it weren't for electrical charges running through our bodies, we wouldn't be alive. It's not much of a stretch that somehow this creature can live without a proper physical form,' Manny said.

Carla looked at him sceptically. 'What does she base this theory on?'

'Tonight when she was at the toyshop, she saw sparks inside of it. And it was more interested in the cars than in the people.' He could see Carla still wasn't convinced. 'Electricity can travel through solid objects. That would explain all the objects it's passed through. It could also explain the fire this morning. The fire-fighter told you it probably started from a short-circuit, right?'

'Okay, suppose that's the case. How does it help us?'

'I don't know yet. But the more we learn the better off we are.'

Manny stood up, leaving Carla on the bench to think some more about what he had said. He crossed the backyard to bring everyone else up to date.

Chapter 15

Later, after checking that Luke was okay and explaining to Cameron and Charlotte everything they had learned at the mall, Grace stood in front of a large map secured to the wall of Manny's lounge room. With all the sightings, the map was starting to look full, and there was no doubt in Grace's mind that the creature was planning to stick around.

She studied the map, trying to memorise the street plan, knowing that if she encountered the creature again her survival might well rest on those details. Though at this stage she was seriously considering never setting foot outside again.

Usually Grace loved her freedom, not having to rely on other people and being able to go where she wanted when she wanted. But living in a town with a monster had made her change a lot of her previously firm beliefs. In this town having no-one to watch your back could get you killed. She felt somehow safer with Manny around. Even with all the other people at his house, people who were all probably very capable, she couldn't help but be thankful he was nearby.

As if reading her mind, Manny appeared at the back door. He crossed the floor and took his place beside her.

'Did you bring Carla up to speed?' she asked.

'Yeah, and everyone in the backyard too. People are really starting to worry.'

For a few moments they lapsed into an uneasy silence. Manny took the time to examine the map. Like Grace, he was alarmed at how much of the city had already been affected by the creature. The three red crosses, each marking a fatality, were particularly concerning, especially considering that the creature had only been around for a day.

'We need to kill this thing,' Manny said. There was no malice in his voice. He was simply stating a fact.

'I've been thinking about that,' Grace admitted. 'Now that we know the creature is made of electricity, surely we can come up with some sort of plan. When anything electrical loses all its energy, it doesn't run anymore. A torch won't work with dead batteries. Isn't there some way we could do that to the creature?'

'Like hook it up to a giant spotlight? There'd be nothing to connect the cables to.'

'What else can we do?'

'We could starve it,' Manny suggested. 'Though I'm no expert, I know how easily electricity can be lost. It must have to eat fairly regularly in order to sustain itself. If we turned off all the electricity in town, it would have to go elsewhere to feed. I'm pretty sure it would starve to death while attempting to cross the desert.'

'I think first it would try to feed on the people here. Each person has a small electrical charge in their body. If there's nothing else available, the creature would go for that. That may be part of the reason it killed the woman in the desert and the other two. If we want to turn off the town's power supply, I think we'd have to evacuate everyone first.'

'There are problems with that. Most people here wouldn't have anywhere else to go. Anyway, this town has thousands of inhabitants. It would take at least a few days to get everybody safely out.'

'Whatever we do, we need to do it quickly. Every day we hesitate will kill more people,' Grace said. 'We know we can't trap it, it will just go through any barriers we put in its way. We have to kill it. But how?' She started pacing across the lounge room then back towards the kitchen. She was talking to herself as much as to Manny. 'We just need to apply ourselves. We know about electricity, and we know about animals. All we have to do is come up with a plan that pulls together all the information we have.' She stopped pacing. 'Metal conducts electricity. Could we skewer the creature with a steel bar and drain the electricity out of it that way?'

'Maybe,' Manny said. 'But you saw it pass through a light-pole. That was metal, right? Did that seem to drain it?'

Grace shrugged. 'No, but it was absorbing the energy out of the light at the same time. It might have been gaining more than it was losing.'

'And I suppose,' Manny said, adding to Grace's train of thought, 'if we were able to stick a piece of metal in it and start to steal its energy, it would realise what was happening and escape.'

'Could we confine it somehow, so it couldn't get away while we drained it?' It didn't occur to her that just moments before she had said caging it would be impossible. 'Maybe there's some way we could increase the amount of energy drained out of it. Is there anything more conductive than metal?'

'Water,' Manny said. 'When you put an electric wire in water, the electricity leaves the wire and goes out into the water, because the water is more conductive.'

Grace took a moment to consider what he had said. He was right of course, but the revelation didn't really help them unless they could come up with some sort of plan to make use of it. She started pacing again.

Manny watched her absently. A few elaborate scenarios played out in his head, but what he really wanted was something simple. 'Maybe we could get a bunch of people together and have them throw buckets of water at the creature,' he suggested.

'It wouldn't work,' Grace said, with close to absolute certainty. 'If the creature targeted them they wouldn't be able to escape.' She continued pacing, making three full laps of the lounge room before she stopped and turned. 'What if we were all up on the rooftops, spraying it with garden hoses? Preferably in a deserted part of town where there's no chance of any innocent bystanders getting hurt. I think one of the warehouses in the industrial district would be our best bet. Although there's still the issue of how to get the creature there.'

'We'd have to lure it,' Manny said. 'Maybe we could set up a generator. We'd just have to ensure there was no other energy nearby to distract it. And the only way to do that would be to cut the whole town's power supply.'

'Could we do that?' Grace asked.

'Carla's father could probably arrange it.' Manny was thoughtful for a minute. 'But there are other problems. The water from a few hoses might not be enough to do the job. What we need is a lot of water. Maybe a fire-truck. If the creature tried to escape we'd be able to follow it. Unless it passed through a wall or something. Plus a fire-truck isn't very manoeuvrable, even at the best of times.' The more he thought about the idea the less practical it became.

'Maybe we're going about this the wrong way,' Grace suggested. 'What if the answer isn't a bit of water that can move around, but a lot of water that's stationary?'

'How do you mean?'

'When I first moved here, I passed the town reservoir on the other side of the mountains. What if we were able to lure the creature onto a boat and then sink the boat? The water in the lake would easily be able to drain all its energy.'

'I don't know. It would be quite an accomplishment to lure the creature that far out of town, especially without getting anyone injured or killed in the process. What we need is a lot of water, but close to the city.'

'Is there any place like that you can think of? Even an empty dam or something that we could pump full of water.'

'How about the town swimming pool?' Manny suggested. 'It's the biggest body of water in the entire city. But the question is, how do we use it? It's not big enough to sink a boat on.'

'It's a pity we can't just get the creature to jump in.'

'Maybe we can,' Manny said thoughtfully. 'What if we put a generator on a raft in the pool? If the electricity was off everywhere else, the creature would have no choice but to go for it. If the raft was right in the middle I don't think the creature could make the jump. If it tried it would be sure to end up in the water, and all the electricity would be drained out of it. Plus I doubt it could move as freely through water as it does through air. It wouldn't escape easily, which means there would be more time for the energy to be sucked out of it.' He looked to Grace for support.

She seemed sceptical. 'Could we arrange something like that?'

'Maybe. I'm more of an ideas man. Carla is the organiser. And she knows a lot about generators and stuff like that. We should run it past her.'

Together they walked into the kitchen. Carla was sitting at the table writing on a small map. She glanced up from her work and saw how serious they both looked.

'What's up?' she asked.

'We have a plan,' Grace announced as both she and Manny took a seat.

Carla looked to Manny and then back at Grace. 'You're not the first ones to say that.'

'This makes a lot of sense,' Manny cut in.

'What exactly?' Carla asked.

'If we turn off the town's electricity supply and put a generator on a raft in the centre of the swimming pool, the creature will be drawn to it. It will have no choice but to jump into the pool to get to the generator. The water should kill it by draining all its energy.'

'What do you think?' Grace asked. 'Is it doable?'

'I don't see why not. All we need is a powerful enough generator to lure it to the pool.' She paused for a moment, deep in thought. 'I know a few people who might be able to help iron out the details. If it all checks out, we should be able to make it work.'

A sound by the door stopped any further discussion. Cameron entered the room with a radio in his hands.

'You guys need to hear this,' he said.

'What is it?' Manny asked.

'I've been keeping in contact with some of my friends who are out on the streets looking for the creature. A few minutes ago the army went to the mall and told everyone to leave the area. They set up a glass greenhouse in the middle of the supermarket parking lot.'

Manny immediately stood up and headed for the front door.

'Where are you going?' Grace asked.

'I want to see this. It proves they know the creature is made of electricity.'

'How can you tell?'

Manny stopped and turned to explain. 'We've seen the creature pass through metal. Metal conducts electricity, which is why the creature can move through it. Glass doesn't conduct electricity. The army plan to get the creature in the greenhouse, and since it can't pass through glass, they should have it trapped.'

'That's why the creature went over the cars in the mall parking lot,' Grace exclaimed. 'It couldn't pass through the windscreens and windows.'

'Probably,' Manny agreed.

'So, what's the plan?' Cameron asked.

'I'm going to drive as close as I can to the supermarket, and then go the rest of the way on foot. The army won't be expecting it, so I should be able to slip in unnoticed. If I can get onto the roof of the mall, I'll be able to keep tabs on what they're up to. If they manage to trap the creature, I want to be the first one to know. And if something goes wrong I may be able to help.'

'And me,' Carla cut in.

'Me too,' said Grace.

Manny looked at them both sceptically. 'Are you sure? It could be dangerous. The creature's certain to be there somewhere, and I don't know how the army will react if they see us.'

'We're sure,' Carla said, speaking for both herself and Grace.

'Would you like me to come too?' asked Cameron.

'No. If there are too many of us, it'll be easier for the army to spot us. You and Charlotte should stay here and hold this place together. Keep in contact with anyone out on the streets. If the creature isn't in the city centre, we need to find out where it is as soon as possible.'

'No problem,' Cameron said.

Manny picked up a walkie-talkie and a torch from the centre of the lounge room. 'With any luck the next time I see you I'll have good news.'

Chapter 16

Fifteen minutes later Manny, Carla and Grace found themselves on the roof of the mall, silently watching what was unfolding.

From their vantage point they had a clear view of the area, even though none of the streetlights in the immediate vicinity were working. Obviously the soldiers had turned them off, along with the electricity for the mall, to ensure the creature didn't arrive before they were ready for it. While it was still likely to be somewhere nearby, the men and women continued their work seemingly fearlessly.

'Do you think this is going to work?' Grace asked, keeping her voice low.

'The army aren't stupid. And they know at least as much as we do,' Manny said. 'My guess is the glass of the greenhouse has been specially made in order to hold the creature. It's probably several times thicker than normal, and it wouldn't surprise me if they've done something to it to make it even less conductive.'

'Could they do that? I mean, it's only been here for a day. Would they have had time to prepare all that?' Grace asked.

'Well, assuming it was at their base all along, they must have known there was the possibility it could escape, and they would have had all this ready just in case. The bigger question is, how do they plan to get the creature into the enclosure? It would be far too dangerous to try to herd it in like cattle.'

Carla leaned forward. 'Take a closer look. There's a generator inside the greenhouse. When they turn it on, the creature should be lured inside.'

'That's no guarantee. The only way to be certain is to make that generator the only source of electricity in the city, or at least the largest.'

'Then that's what they'll do,' Carla said. 'When they're ready, they'll cut the city's power and the creature will have no choice but to go for the generator.' She rubbed her hands together, attempting to keep the chill of the night at bay.

At that moment a change seemed to flow through the group assembled in the parking lot. While most of the personnel withdrew to the relative safety of the mall, a solitary figure entered the greenhouse. A dull roar began to emanate from within. The soldier had started the generator. He left the structure and ran towards the buildings. Enormous sparks bounced off the interior of the enclosure.

'It looks like they're ready to start,' Manny said.

Suddenly all the lights in the city seemed to fail at once, cloaking the town in darkness. Grace, already on the edge because of what they were doing, almost lost her composure. A brief, calming touch from Manny helped her to keep her cool.

'It's okay,' Manny said quietly. 'Everything is going according to plan. That generator is now the only source of electricity in Carlton. The creature is sure to be interested in it.'

Carla looked over her shoulder and scanned the rooftop. 'Manny, I think I'll go to the other side of the roof, above the Food Mart stockrooms. That's probably where the creature will come from, since that's where you last saw it.'

'Good idea,' Manny said. 'I'll stay here and keep an eye on things.'

'Grace can stay with you,' Carla whispered. 'If the creature comes from another direction, one of you will be able to run over and let me know.'

'Okay,' he agreed.

Carla set off for the far side of the mall, leaving Manny and Grace to watch over the parking lot. Manny sat down and rested his chin on the small barrier that encircled the roof, while Grace took a seat on a raised air vent.

There were hardly any stars in the sky, and the moon was hidden behind the clouds. In fact, the only light came from the sparks jumping off the generator and bouncing around inside the greenhouse. Grace looked across at Manny, his face flickering faintly in the light of the sparks. He seemed lost in thought and she couldn't help but wonder what was going on in his head.

'It sure is dark,' she said, her voice little more than a whisper.

A second passed without a reply and Grace worried she had annoyed him by speaking without good reason.

'You'll get used to it after a while,' Manny said. He sounded relieved that she had broken the silence.

'When we talked about this earlier, you made it seem a lot more exciting than it really is.'

'It was all part of my plan to get you out here,' he teased. 'If you hadn't come with me tonight I'd be sitting here alone, with no-one but myself to talk to.'

Grace was suddenly embarrassed and didn't know why. She hoped Manny couldn't hear it in her voice. 'How long do you think it will be before the creature shows up?' she asked.

'I don't know. I guess it depends on how far away it is, and how often it needs to recharge its energy. I assume it has to eat fairly regularly. We shouldn't have to wait too long.' He paused, and for a moment Grace thought he wasn't going to say any more, but then he spoke again. It was completely off the topic, but she didn't mind. 'How do you like it here? In this town, I mean. Being the new kid and all?'

Grace didn't answer right away. Instead she scanned the parking lot as she gathered her thoughts. 'I liked it a lot more before the creature arrived,' she said, somewhat regretfully. 'And even though I'm new, I'm certainly not a kid. I think I proved that tonight.'

'Don't be so quick to condemn it. Once you lose your childhood, you can't ever get it back.'

'I'm surprised you didn't give up your innocence a long time ago.'

Manny smiled, secure in the knowledge that Grace would never see it. 'My childlike ingenuity and enthusiasm have gotten me out of more scrapes than I'd care to remember.'

'I think it was probably your childish enthusiasm that got you into the scrapes in the first place,' Grace countered.

Manny chuckled softly. 'Maybe.'

'Maybe not,' Grace said, remembering what he had done earlier at the mall. He had put himself in danger in an attempt to save the life of a stranger. His efforts hadn't been successful, but at least he tried, and now they knew exactly how the creature killed people. She changed the subject again. 'What do you think the army will do with the creature when they catch it?'

Manny answered without hesitation. 'Study it.'

'You don't think they'll try to kill it? If it escaped from them once, there's nothing to ensure it wouldn't happen again,' she said.

'I don't know. Maybe this time they'll be more careful. But I think if they intended to kill it, they wouldn't bother trying to trap it first. They would kill it outright.'

'Unless they don't know how,' Grace suggested. 'They may have all those high-tech gadgets, and be looking for a high-tech solution, whereas we have very few resources to work with, leaving us no choice but to make our idea simple.' She paused. 'Still, even if they can't kill it, at least if they trap it we won't have to worry about it anymore.'

'Maybe it's for the best if they don't succeed.'

'What do you mean?' Grace asked.

'If they can trap it, it means we've lost our shot at trying to kill it. I'd sleep a lot easier knowing it was dead rather than just locked away in some government research laboratory. And not only because it could escape again. If the army had it, they had it for a reason. And I don't think they were studying it for the next medical breakthrough. What if they want to use it to develop some sort of energy weapon? We know the creature kills with a touch. What if they were able to replicate that? It has the potential to change the balance of power in the world. Imagine if it fell into the wrong hands.'

Grace shifted her position slightly. 'How can they study something that can pass through solid matter? They probably just want to contain it until they can figure out a way to destroy it.'

'Assuming they had it captured before, it could have been there for years. They would have had plenty of chances to kill it if that's what they intended. What I'd really like to know is how they captured it in the first place. Or perhaps they didn't capture it. Maybe they made it.'

'You think they could have created it?' Grace asked, incredulous. 'Why would they? The risk of something like that would be enormous.'

Manny looked over at Grace's shadowy form. She almost managed to make the idea seem absurd. But the idea of an invisible, incorporeal creature prowling the streets was absurd too, and it was as real as everything else.

Grace took his silence to mean he was considering what she had said. She continued, 'You know the creature as well as anyone. Would it even be possible to engineer something like that?'

'I don't know,' Manny admitted, 'but I can't see it happening naturally either.' He leaned back, tilting his head towards the sky. The cloud cover was almost complete. For a moment his thoughts returned to previous night, and the way the creature had seemed bothered by the rain. Yet more proof that it didn't like water. In fact, in the end, Manny was sure it was no longer chasing them, but just looking for a way out of the storm.

The sound of footsteps echoed across the roof, interrupting Manny's reverie. Carla had abandoned her position on the far side of the building.

'I saw the creature. It's coming in this direction.'

'Where?' Manny asked.

'Just down the street. It won't be long.'

The three of them pressed against the edge of the building as they waited for the creature to appear.

A minute later, just as Carla had predicted, it emerged from around the side of the mall. It paused for a moment, scanning the area, then crossed the parking lot and approached the greenhouse, obviously drawn by the energy from the generator.

It cautiously circled the structure as if sensing something was wrong. Manny held his breath. Despite what he had said only moments before, he genuinely hoped the army would be successful in their attempt.

Finally deciding there was nothing to worry about, the creature stepped into the enclosure.

As soon as it crossed the threshold a door slid across, trapping it within. At the same moment someone shut off the generator using a remote control. Immediately the creature became agitated. It moved backwards and forwards in the limited confines of the structure as if searching for a way past the barriers.

It did this several times, and with each passing moment became even more desperate.

It pushed at the walls, trying to shift them, then, when it could not, it started to move through the glass; slowly at first, but then much faster. In moments it was standing outside the greenhouse.

Now free of the enclosure, there was nothing cautious about the creature. It bounded across the parking lot and disappeared into the darkness.

The army had come close, Manny realised. They had almost succeeded. Another inch or two of glass and perhaps the creature would have been trapped.

'What now?' Grace asked.

Manny looked over the parking lot one last time. 'There's nothing more we can do here. I think we should return to my house and try to get some rest.'

Chapter 17

After arriving back at Manny's house and reporting everything that had happened during the army's attempt to capture the creature, the hopeful mood that had been present rapidly deteriorated.

The gathered group quickly shrank until only a few remained; Charlotte and two others whose names Manny couldn't remember. Even Luke and Cameron had left, deciding to risk a trip to the Emergency Department. Manny's mother failed to return, though she called from the hospital to say she would be staying the night in case there was a sudden rush of injuries because of the creature. Manny didn't have the heart to tell her that any physical contact with it seemed to be fatal.

The city's power was still off, leaving the creature no choice but to prey on the townspeople if it wanted to feed. In order to keep everyone safe, Manny came up with the idea to position generators around the city as an alternate food-source.

By this stage it was nearing midnight, and everyone was feeling weary.

Charlotte suggested that Manny, Grace and Carla get some rest while she and the other two kept lookout from the roof and stayed in contact with the few brave souls who were still trying to track the creature. She reasoned that while Manny and the girls had been running around town keeping an eye on the army, she and the others had the enviable position of staying comfortable at Manny's house, so it made sense that they should take the first watch.

Manny and Carla set up two sleeping bags in the lounge room while Grace took the couch. If something happened, all three could quickly be raised from slumber. They each slept fitfully for a few hours.

Eventually Manny was gently awakened by Charlotte.

'Manny, the others and I are pretty beat. We've thought about it and decided it's time to finish up for the night. A few minutes ago I called around to anyone we have keeping an eye out for the creature, but no-one has seen it. The guys watching over the generators you suggested have just changed shifts, and none of them have caught sight of it either. From what I can tell, there haven't been any encounters since the army failed to catch it. I don't think anything else is likely to happen tonight, but I thought I'd wake you in case you wanted to monitor the radios.'

'Thanks,' Manny said. 'What time is it?'

'About three-thirty.'

'Okay. You and the others can go home. Remember, we're all meeting at the college tomorrow. At some point after twelve so everyone has a chance to get some sleep.'

Charlotte and the other two left as Manny pulled up a chair at the kitchen table. He stayed there for more than ten minutes, trying to wrap his head around everything that was happening. Just as Charlotte had predicted, the radios stayed silent.

Around the room, several candles burned, evidence that the army still hadn't turned on the city's power supply.

Manny was jolted from his thoughts as Grace came up beside him. 'What time is it?' she asked.

'About twenty-to-four.'

'How long have you been sitting here?'

'Only a few minutes. Charlotte and the others wanted to leave, so she woke me up.'

'You should have woken me as well.'

'And me,' Carla said, coming in from the lounge and joining the other two at the table.

Manny took the opportunity to update them on the information he had received from Charlotte and for the next few minutes no-one said a word.

Realising that sitting there was doing nothing to lessen her anxiety, Carla stood up and started pacing the room. Manny and Grace watched intently.

'We can't keep going like this,' Carla said.

Manny stretched a little in his seat. 'We don't have a choice. As long as this thing is around we have to do everything we can to keep the townspeople safe. When we're ready, we'll try the pool plan. Until then all we can do is our best.'

'I'm not sure that will be enough. You saw tonight how bad it is. Even the army can't hold this thing. How are we supposed to stop it?'

'Our idea is going to work,' Manny said, 'and if it doesn't, well, we'll just have to come up with another plan. Something better.'

Grace regarded him carefully. 'We're out of our depth here, Manny. I think it's time we seriously considered evacuating the town. Even if the army won't officially admit it, everyone knows what's going on, especially the police. Surely if we went to them they'd be able to arrange something. I'm certain Carla's father would help us.'

'I'm not convinced it's reached that stage yet. If there was an evacuation, it could cause a panic. People might die.'

'People have already died, and if we don't act now, it's only a matter of time until more do.'

'As far as we know, the creature doesn't like going through walls. When it was trapped earlier it only did it as a last resort. People should be safe as long as they stay in their houses,' Manny said.

'But that wall was glass,' Grace reminded him, 'and the creature managed to pass through, even though it wasn't supposed to be able to. I'm guessing wooden or brick walls aren't going to slow it down either. If it wants to be inside, I don't think there's any way to prevent it. Evacuating is the only sensible option.'

'There's still the problem of where to relocate everyone. Most of them have nowhere to go.'

'I've been thinking about that,' Carla put in. 'So far the creature has stayed within the city limits, probably because it would lose too much energy if it tried to cross the desert. We could set up a temporary city of tents, caravans and motor-homes on the other side of the mountains. It's far enough away that if the creature tried to get there it would be sure to starve to death.'

'I think we should try the pool idea first. If it's successful we won't have to move anybody anywhere,' said Manny.

Grace wasn't convinced. 'I don't think we can risk it. A creature made of electricity is unheard of. I'm guessing that the more energy it absorbs, the faster and stronger it will become. I'd like to move everyone as far away as possible – and the sooner the better.'

'Relocating a population of this size is going to be a big undertaking. It'll take at least a few days to see if it's viable, then more time to get things moving. I'm not even sure we'll be able to find enough tents and caravans for everyone,' Manny said.

'Maybe the army could help with housing,' Grace suggested. 'They have plenty of tents set up in the city centre.'

'That's a long shot,' Manny said. 'How are we going to convince them to help us when they won't even admit that the creature exists? I think the pool plan is our best bet.'

Realising they were starting to go around in circles, Carla took control. 'How about a compromise,' she suggested. 'We'll work on both ideas, and try whichever comes together first.'

'That sounds alright,' Manny said.

'Couldn't hurt,' Grace agreed.

'Now all we need is a way to keep the creature out of our hair long enough to get things ready. We can't have it running around town while the electricity is off. Even with the generators we've set up to keep it busy, I'm not completely comfortable. If they break down the only food-source for the creature will be the townspeople.'

'We could set up a generator out in the desert in order to lure the creature away,' Grace suggested. 'That would make the town even safer.'

Carla shrugged. 'It's not something we could do tonight, but I think I could manage it tomorrow. We'd need a lot of power to attract the creature, and a generator like that would be large and difficult to shift, but aside from that I think it would be doable.'

'What about the one at the airport?'

'Maybe. It's definitely big enough, but my guess is it's too far out of town for the creature to sense. And moving it closer would be almost impossible,' Carla said. 'I think a better idea would be a smaller generator set up close to the city. Or maybe we could arrange a few generators in a line to lure the creature out to the airport.'

'I'm starting to feel better,' Manny said. 'We have a Plan A and a Plan B, even if we're not sure which is which yet, and a few other possibilities. What more do we need?'

'Information would be nice,' Grace said. 'So far everything we know about the creature is pretty much a wild guess. Unfortunately, the army are the only ones who have the data we need, and no matter how nicely we ask, there's no way they'll just hand it over.'

'It couldn't hurt to try,' Manny said. 'Given that the creature escaped their trap, they may not be thinking straight. We might not get a better opportunity to find out what they know. I could swing by the city centre and try talking with Colonel Markham. If I leave now we could have all the information we need before the sun comes up.'

Carla was hesitant. 'That could be dangerous. We have no idea where the creature is. No-one has seen it since the army's plan failed. It hasn't been to any of our generators, and with the electricity off everywhere else it's guaranteed to be hungry. Even a car battery is likely to attract it at this stage.'

'Carla is right,' Grace agreed. 'We need information and any help they can give us, but it can wait until morning. It'll be safer then.'

'I don't think we can afford to postpone it,' Manny said, pulling his backpack onto his shoulders.

'We should send someone else,' Carla pleaded. 'Someone who lives closer to the temporary base. The less distance to travel means less chance of running into the creature.'

'No, it has to be me. I already have a history with Colonel Markham.'

Carla sighed. 'Do you need any help?'

'No. You two stay here. Start making a list of things we need for an evacuation. Then when morning comes you can take it to your father. If we're lucky, preparations may be able to start right away.'

Grace wasn't convinced. 'You'll be heading to the centre of town, where the creature was last seen. You're still tired. If it attacks, you might not be able to outrun it. At least if one of us went with you it would be an extra set of eyes.'

'I'll be fine,' Manny said. 'I had enough sleep to replenish my energy. Plus, there's a lot of easy access to the roofs in that part of town. If something does go wrong I shouldn't have any problem making it to safety. And I'll take a radio. If I run into trouble I can call someone nearby for help.'

Seeing that there was no way to convince him to wait, Grace asked, 'Is there anything else you want us to do here?'

'Yeah. Stay in touch with anyone still looking for the creature. If I'm going to be in the centre of town, I'd prefer to know that it was somewhere else.' He started towards the front door.

'Be careful,' Grace told him.

Manny nodded, then left the house.

Chapter 18

The sky was still dark as Manny pulled to a stop in front of the university, even though sunrise was less than an hour away. He climbed from his jeep and crossed the road to the army's temporary headquarters. He expected to be challenged at the entrance, but there was no-one around. Even stranger, the gate had been left wide open.

He looked along the street. The previous morning, when he had been summoned there with Carla, the spaces had been occupied by dozens of army vehicles. Now they were all vacant.

For a moment Manny wondered if everyone was still at the mall. But that didn't make any sense since that operation had finished hours ago. He quickly dismissed the idea. Even if most of the soldiers were elsewhere, they would have at least left some guards behind.

He walked through the gateway and entered the closest tent. A lamp illuminated everything inside. A brief, disturbing thought brushed at the edges of Manny's mind, but he couldn't quite catch it. Instead he examined the interior. There wasn't much to see. Two tables strewn with paper, four chairs and a small filing cabinet with the lamp on top. It was a multi-person office, yet aside from himself there was no-one present.

He left the tent and looked towards the centre of the compound.

It was clear to Manny, even without going further in, that the entire camp was deserted. He assumed the army had withdrawn to their base out of town. That wouldn't happen unless something had gone very wrong. There was only one explanation. The creature had been there. Nothing else could make the army vacate their position so quickly.

He was about to turn and leave when he realised what a unique opportunity he had been presented with. Surely somewhere in the camp there would be information about the creature. All he had to do was find it. He guessed the most likely spot for it would be in some of the larger tents towards the centre of the camp.

Before he could begin his search, he remembered the lamp in the tent. The army had a generator running somewhere, and it was one of the few sources of electricity in Carlton. In fact, before Manny had organised for other generators to be set up, this base would have been the only food-source for the creature in the entire city. After almost being captured at the mall, it had probably went to the base straight away to make up its lost energy.

Manny began to worry. Assuming the creature had eaten several hours ago, it would probably be hungry again soon. He didn't want it to reappear during his search. With other generators now active around the city, he could safely shut this one down without placing the townspeople on the menu.

He knew he would find the generator in a tent somewhere in the middle of the compound. Turning it off had to be his first priority, especially if he was going to be there for a while, but he couldn't quite bring himself to go that way yet.

The camp was an unnerving place at night, and it had little to do with the darkness. It was the silence. Without the chatter of the soldiers the temporary base seemed completely alien.

But, he realised, it wasn't just the camp that was silent. It was as if the whole town had gone to sleep. There was no noise anywhere, not even any barking dogs. The night was as still as any he could remember. Most people were confined to their houses, probably sleeping the night away. Everyone else was keeping a quiet lookout for the creature from the safety of the rooftops, sitting around a radio listening for some clue as to what was going on outside, or, in the case of a few brave souls, actually walking the streets.

Manny approached the next tent and stepped inside. It too was empty. There was no lamp here and the room lay in darkness. He lifted up the tent flap and allowed some moonlight to penetrate, but even that wasn't enough. Using the key-ring torch from his pocket he examined the area.

A table and chairs sat in the centre of the tent, with a portable filing cabinet off to the side. One of the drawers had been knocked to the floor, and now papers were scattered across the ground. Manny picked up a few pages and quickly scanned them but couldn't see anything worthwhile.

He set them down on the table and carefully manoeuvred around the other pieces of furniture in the tent. Even with the light from his torch, the room was dark and unsettling. He moved almost silently, listening for any sound other than his own quiet breathing.

Nearby, something scraped against the hard canvas of a tent.

Without even stopping to think, Manny turned off his torch, squatted down behind the desk and pushed himself against it.

He looked around for something he could use to defend himself if the need arose but couldn't see anything that would prove handy as a weapon. Instead he grabbed the chair from beside him and waited.

He heard the light footfalls as two individuals entered the tent. They seemed cautious, walking close together and almost clinging to each other for support. Unlike Manny, they didn't appear to have a torch. One of them approached the desk and pulled on the chair. Manny abruptly stood up, his hands grasping the back of the seat.

'Hey,' he called, not sure what else he could say.

Grace and Carla jumped back, each barely suppressing a scream.

Manny recognised them immediately and let go of the chair. 'What are you two doing here?' he asked, both thankful for the company and annoyed that they had put themselves in harm's way.

'We came to see if you needed any help,' Carla answered.

'I nearly knocked you both unconscious,' Manny explained regretfully.

'That's a risk we were willing to take,' Grace said.

'You wouldn't be so forgiving if you were lying on the floor right now.'

Grace shrugged her shoulders. 'If we were lying on the floor right now we wouldn't be having this conversation.'

'You know I asked you to stay back at the house for a reason.'

'Planning the evacuation can wait a few hours. We thought you might need some help convincing Colonel Markham to give us the information,' Grace said.

'And we both knew the only reason you didn't want us here was so you wouldn't be endangering us,' Carla added.

'Yeah,' Manny agreed sarcastically. 'What was I thinking?'

Carla ignored him and instead asked, 'Why were you hiding?'

'I didn't hear your car,' Manny said, still feeling guilty about almost hitting them with a chair. 'I didn't realise it was you. I thought it might have been the soldiers returning.'

'We parked on the other side of the oval and came in the gate there. It was wide open with no-one guarding it. I think the entire camp has been deserted.'

'That's what I thought too. And the only reason they would do that was if the creature came here.'

'That sounds like a good guess,' Carla said, switching on her torch and scanning the room.

'How soon after I left did you two start following me?' Manny asked.

'Only a minute or two,' Grace answered. 'When we came here and saw that the place was deserted we were worried we wouldn't be able to find you, but then we saw your light between the tents, so we came straight over.' She flipped idly through a few of the papers on the table.

'I already checked those,' Manny told her. 'I didn't find anything useful. I figure they probably keep all the good stuff in the tents closer to the centre of the oval. That's where I was planning to go next. Plus, the army has a generator running somewhere, and it has to be shut off. If the creature has come and gone, we don't want to give it any reason to come back.'

'Sounds like a good idea,' Carla said.

Together the three left the tent and hurried towards the middle of the compound. Manny led the way as Carla and Grace huddled closely behind him. He almost wished they hadn't assumed he would take the lead. It wasn't his intention to lead them into danger, but he realised that could be exactly what he was doing.

As they travelled deeper into the camp, the tell-tale purr of the generator grew louder. Manny followed the noise to a nearby tent. He pulled aside the flap and shone his torch through the opening. When he was convinced it was safe he slipped inside, followed by the two girls a moment later.

He took Carla's torch – it was brighter than his own – and used it to examine the machine in front of him. He found the off switch and pressed it. The generator fell silent.

Manny began to relax. Without the electricity to draw it, there was no reason for the creature to return, and the three of them could safely search the camp for the information they required.

He headed for a door on the far side of the tent and once more stepped out into the night. Carla and Grace stayed close behind him.

As they walked their footfalls barely made a sound. At first Manny thought they were all unconsciously trying to be quiet, then he realised it was because they were walking on the soft grass of the university oval. The strangeness of the environment had almost made him forget that he was in a place so familiar to him.

He continued towards the centre of the camp, eager to get the search over with, but suddenly came to a stop.

In the circle of light made by Carla's torch was a boot. And attached to the boot was a body.

'Hold this,' Manny said, handing the flashlight to Carla. He hurried over to see if anything could be done.

Though the soldier was face down, Manny could tell it was a man not too much older than himself. He knelt down and checked for a pulse. There was none and the body was cold to the touch. He guessed the soldier had been dead for several hours, confirming his suspicion that the creature had been there immediately after escaping the trap at the mall. Every instinct within Manny told him to start CPR, but he knew it wouldn't do any good. Even if the victim had died only a minute ago, a touch from the creature meant instant, irrevocable death.

Manny stood up, thankful he hadn't seen the person's face.

He carefully stepped around the body, then directed the girls to do the same. He took the flashlight back from Carla and handed her the key-ring torch he had been using earlier.

With unspoken agreement they all moved forward, as if increasing their distance from the body would somehow allow them to forget what they had seen, but before they had even gone ten metres, Manny paused again.

'What is it?' Carla asked.

Manny held up his hand to silence her.

'I heard something,' he whispered.

Carla listened carefully. She couldn't hear anything, but she trusted Manny's ears as well as his judgement.

'Where?' she mouthed.

He pointed at a pile of crates sitting a few metres in front of them. Manny motioned for the two girls to stay back, then cautiously approached. As he rounded the crates he saw someone lying on the ground. It took him a moment to recognise Colonel Markham, the man who had interviewed him that morning.

Grace was by the colonel's side a moment later. 'We're here to help,' she said.

Manny noticed Carla slip away. He didn't know where she was going but he knew she could handle herself.

'How is everyone else?' Colonel Markham asked. He coughed painfully as he tried to sit up.

Manny didn't have the heart to tell him about the body they had found. 'They escaped,' he said.

'What happened here?' Grace asked.

'The creature breached the perimeter fence. Someone raised the alarm. Everyone started to panic. I realised it was coming for the generator so I tried to shut it off but was trampled in the rush.' He coughed again. 'What are you doing here?'

Manny decided a quick explanation was best. 'We need information about the creature in order to kill it. And any help you can give us in evacuating the town.'

Before the colonel could answer, Carla reappeared, her mobile phone in her hands. 'I called the hospital. There's an ambulance on the way. I told them where we are and what's happened.'

Manny turned his attention back to Colonel Markham, but he'd already slipped into unconsciousness. They stayed by his side for the next five minutes, waiting for the ambulance to arrive.

Once the colonel was safely on his way to hospital, Manny escorted Carla and Grace back to Carla's car, then he returned to his jeep on the far side of the oval so he could finally go home and get some sleep.

Chapter 19

Manny was waiting in front of the college, thinking about how strange it felt to be at school on a Sunday, especially since he had only gotten out of bed a few minutes earlier, when Carla arrived in her convertible.

'Good morning,' Manny said. Then he checked his watch and corrected, 'Afternoon.'

Carla smiled as she climbed out of her car. 'I was going to ask how you were doing, but I see your body clock is just as screwed up as mine.' She looked him over carefully. 'How much sleep did you get?'

'Not as much as I needed. I had trouble getting myself out of bed earlier, but I don't feel so bad now.'

'I know what you mean,' Carla said. 'I had a killer headache when I woke up. Luckily it's starting to recede.'

Manny was instantly concerned. 'You should go home. I'm sure we can get by without you.'

Carla looked annoyed. It bothered her that Manny always had her best interests at heart, but seemed to disregard his own. 'I'm fine. And I'm needed more here.'

Before they could say anything else, Grace appeared at the main doors of the college. She smiled and waved them over.

'I didn't think you had arrived yet,' Manny said.

'I woke up at ten-thirty and knew I wouldn't get back to sleep, so I came here. I figured there was bound to be something I could do. The biology majors are on the second floor trying to figure out the creature's physiology, the engineering students are in the workshop getting the generator ready, and everyone else is either strategizing for the operation tonight or planning the evacuation. Charlotte has me running errands and co-ordinating between the various groups. We also still have people situated across the city keeping watch for the creature, but no-one's seen it yet.'

'How's the pool plan going?' Carla asked.

'Everything seems to be on track. There was a vote earlier, and it was decided that tonight will be the best time to take our shot. The idea is to start just after sundown so there will be fewer spectators around. There have been a few issues with the generator, but the engineering students are confident it'll be ready in time.'

'What about the evacuation?'

'We're doing what we can, but it's been difficult to find supplies. The desert gets freezing at night, and even a tent and sleeping bag won't be much help. Even so, Charlotte arranged for a group of students to take down the tents left behind by the army. They're being carted to a place on the other side of the mountains, so we have the option if we need it. Everyone agrees the spot they've chosen is far enough away to be safe from the creature, but until we can deal with the temperature issue, an evacuation just won't be possible.' Grace seemed disappointed that their backup plan was no longer an option.

'At the moment there isn't much else we can do,' Carla said gently. 'Anyway, if the plan tonight works the way we think it will, there won't be any need for an evacuation.'

'And even if it doesn't,' Manny added, 'we'll still have some time to plot our next move.'

'I hope you're right,' Grace said uneasily, glancing across the street at the temporary base.

Manny followed her gaze. Several college students sat around a table, carefully reading through files left behind by the army. Judging by the number of discarded boxes sitting a few metres away, the group had probably been there all morning.

'According to Charlotte, they started as soon as the police were done searching the camp for any other casualties,' Grace said, seemingly reading Manny's mind.

'Have they managed to find any new information?' he asked.

'Not a lot,' Grace admitted. 'Most of the data seems to be about the army's plan to capture the creature in the mall parking lot, rather than what it is or how it came to exist.' She checked her watch. 'I should go. Charlotte asked me to get some books from the library, and I've kept her waiting long enough.'

'I'll go with you,' Manny volunteered.

Carla looked towards the school buildings. 'I have some things to do too. I want to check in with the students at the garage to see how things are progressing with the generator, then I might visit Luke at the hospital.' She turned and headed for the engineering workshop as Manny and Grace started towards the library.

A minute later they entered through the main doors. A young woman was waiting for them and handed Grace a stack of books.

'I think this is everything Charlotte was after, but if not let me know.' With that she hurried away on some other errand.

'What are all these?' Manny asked, indicating the books Grace had been given.

'They're to do with animal psychology. Even though the creature is radically different physically from every other animal on the planet, we're hoping it will share the same basic behaviour. If we can figure out how it thinks, it may give us a valuable advantage.'

As she turned to leave, Manny caught her arm. 'You had even less sleep last night than I did. You didn't have to come in today.'

Grace was touched by his concern. 'I want to be a part of this.'

'You've already helped us more than you can imagine. You were the one who figured out the creature is made of energy.'

'I wasn't the first to realise it. The army knew all along. They just didn't clue anyone else in.'

She pushed open the door and together they left the library.

'Are you going back to Charlotte now?' Manny asked.

'That's the plan. What about you?'

'There's a meeting I should be at shortly, but I still have a bit of time. After that I want to see Colonel Markham at the hospital. He's recovering from surgery at the moment so I'm waiting for a call to let me know he's ready to receive visitors. I'm hoping to get a bit more information out of him. Until then I think I should hang around here in case something comes up. Everyone knows about the guy killed at the mall and the soldier who died. Even though it doesn't seem like it, people are panicking.' He paused for a moment. 'It's weird being here today; knowing someone was killed just across the street.'

'Don't think about it,' Grace said, changing the subject so she could follow her own advice. 'Do you want to meet somewhere before the pool plan starts?'

'I don't know. I'm not really sure what I'll be doing this afternoon. If you like I can give you a call later on and we can figure something out.'

'Sounds good.'

They crossed the courtyard and entered the largest school building through a side door. A young man rushed up to Manny and handed him a blue folder.

'What's this?' Manny asked.

'It's the specifics of the generator we're going to use tonight. We've been in a meeting all morning trying to decide what will work best. Michelle wants your opinion before the end of the day.'

Manny opened the folder and saw a stack of schematic diagrams. 'This really isn't my area of expertise,' he said.

'It doesn't matter. Just take a look and let her know what you think.' The student ran off on some other mission.

Manny and Grace climbed the stairs to the second floor. Another student approached.

'Have you got the specifics from Michelle yet?' the young woman asked.

Manny held up the folder. 'Right here,' he said.

'Good.' She handed him another folder. 'This is all the non-technical stuff. What buildings we'll be using, where people will be located when it happens, all that sort of stuff.'

Manny took a quick look inside the folder. 'Who do I see about this?'

'Whoever is in charge tonight. I think it's Kathryn, but I may be wrong. If there's a major problem, come by a bit early. That way we can sort it out before the sun goes down.' She hurried away.

Manny watched her go and then turned back to Grace. 'I don't understand why everyone wants my input. I don't know any more than they do.'

'I guess it's because you organised everything last night,' Grace said.

'Actually that was mostly Carla.'

'True, but it was your house.'

Manny held the classroom door for Grace as she stepped inside, then he headed off for the meeting he had promised to attend.

Chapter 20

Later that afternoon Manny received the call telling him to stop by the hospital. His first priority was to talk to his mother, who he hadn't seen since before the creature arrived.

After a few minutes with her, Manny went to see Luke. He had a minor concussion but was going to be fine. The doctors had decided to keep him under observation for a few more hours, though he would be released by the end of the day. Manny learned that Carla and Cameron had stopped by earlier too.

Finally Manny entered the private wards where Colonel Markham was being treated. He was sitting in a bed, propped up by several pillows.

'How are you feeling?' Manny asked, taking a seat beside the bed.

'Better than can be expected. I was in surgery this morning to stop some internal bleeding, but the doctors don't think there's any permanent damage.'

'You were lucky we came by when we did.'

'It's a shame that's not the case for everyone,' the colonel said. 'Were any more fatalities discovered?' Manny guessed one of the nurses must have told him about the body.

'No. The police did a thorough search early this morning and didn't find anyone else. As far as I know they checked the whole camp. Unfortunately all of your men seem to have left town so we can't do a proper head-count.'

'That doesn't surprise me. In case of an emergency they were told to regroup at the base out of town.'

Colonel Markham lay back on the pillows and sighed. The chart beside the bed indicated he was on pain medication. He was lucid now, but there was no telling how long it would last. Manny decided it was time to get down to business. 'Are there any weapons capable of killing the creature?' he asked.

'No. Nothing like that.'

'What about ways to repel it, or to contain it.'

The colonel shut his eyes for a moment. 'How much do you know about the creature?'

'We know it's made of electricity, but that's about all.'

Colonel Markham nodded and began to explain. 'About four years ago a severe lightning storm struck near the base. You might even remember it. Some of our soldiers were testing a newly-developed energy weapon, similar to a taser, only much more powerful. One of the men thought it might be fun to use it on bear that lived in the area. When the current hit the animal, something happened. Our scientists think it was due to a combination of the charge from the weapon and the ambient energy from the thunderstorm. All the electrical impulses that were running through the bear's body were somehow moved outside of it. The bear's body died, but the impulses stayed active.'

The colonel paused for a moment to take a sip of water from a glass on the bedside table. He set the glass down again and continued with his story.

'The area where this happened was surrounded by a fence with an electro-magnetic field running through it. The idea was that the field would neutralise any stray energy bolts that missed the target. We came to realise that what remained of the animal was unable to pass through the field. With a bit of difficulty we were able to lure the creature inside our facility and trap it in a specially-built containment cell. We've had it imprisoned ever since, but on Friday, somehow it managed to escape. At that point it was still trapped within the compound, because the external fence had a stronger electro-magnetic field running through it, but one of our technicians disabled the field and released the creature in order to prevent it killing the people trapped inside the base with it.'

'Probably the right decision,' Manny grudgingly admitted.

'Last night, we built a glass enclosure at the mall. Since the creature is made of energy, we reasoned that once it was inside the structure, it wouldn't be able to escape because glass doesn't conduct electricity. But that didn't turn out to be correct. While the operation was happening at the mall, I was back at the temporary base watching everything remotely. We had a generator set up to run our equipment. I guess the creature lost a lot of energy escaping our trap, and since all the other electricity in the city was turned off, it had no choice but to go for the generator at the temporary base. We didn't think the creature would be able to get to it because there was an electro-magnetic field running through the perimeter fence. The gate was shut and the field was at full power, but the creature still got inside.'

'So we can assume that the creature has somehow adapted to it,' Manny surmised.

'That's what it looks like. But from what we can tell, the field running through the external fence at the base out of town is still strong enough to hold it. It has something to do with the length of the fence allowing the particles to reach a higher speed.'

'Could we lead the creature back to the base and trap it inside?'

'It's possible, but my bosses would never go for it. And even if they did, there's no way to guarantee it wouldn't just escape again. It's already adapted to the weaker fields, so it's probably only a matter of time before it's able to adapt to the stronger field. I think the only way to ensure everyone's safety is to kill it.'

'And if we can't?'

'The army will find a way to trap it, no matter how long it takes. Already the higher-ups are talking about bringing in a more powerful electro-magnetic field generator to power the original containment cell. Even with everything that's happened, they still want it alive. Something like this has the capacity to change the world.'

'Why are you telling me this?'

'I think you've earned the right to hear the truth. The army are going to regroup, and then they'll try to recapture it. At most, you have twenty-four hours before they flood this town with equipment and personnel. You'll only have one shot to kill it. I've spent most of the morning trying to devise a plan. The best I could come up with was to get a fire-truck to train its hoses on the creature. If you were able to follow it for long enough, never letting it out of the stream of water, I think that would do the trick.'

It was a small comfort to Manny that someone who knew the creature so much better than himself had produced a plan vaguely similar to his own. 'I'll talk to some people I know and see if it's possible,' he said, instinctively choosing not to tell the colonel about their alternate idea. There wasn't really any logic behind it, except that perhaps Manny still didn't quite trust him because of what had happened at their initial meeting.

The colonel smiled weakly then lay back in the bed and closed his eyes.

Realising that he had learned all he could for the moment, Manny decided it was time to leave. The doctors at the hospital would ensure Colonel Markham received the best care available, but right now what he probably needed more than anything else was a good night's sleep to regain his strength.

Manny stood up and headed for the door. He turned back one final time and was pleased to see the colonel had slipped into peaceful slumber. Manny quietly left the room.

Outside the main entrance of the hospital he was surprised to find one of the army technicians waiting for him.

'You're Immanuel Logan, right?' the man asked.

'That's right,' Manny said, 'and you are...?'

'My name is Gavin Powell. I'm the technician from the army base who released the creature.'

'Colonel Markham told me about that. From what I can tell you didn't have much of a choice.'

'That may be right,' Gavin said, 'but I still can't help feeling responsible for the people it's killed.'

There wasn't anything Manny could say that would change Gavin's mind, so instead he asked, 'Are you here to see the colonel? He was sleeping when I left him.'

'Actually I'm here to see you. I've had a hell of a time tracking you down. I've been trying to come up with a way to stop the creature. It was originally contained in an electro-magnetic field at the army base, but it managed to escape. It was also able to pass through a similar field at the temporary base last night. But I think the field in the perimeter fence at the military base is still strong enough to hold it.' It was a repeat of the information he had just received from Colonel Markham, but Manny didn't interrupt. 'If we can lure the creature back there we might be able to trap it inside again. That should buy us some time at least. The only thing is, all the army officers are back there currently, so we'd need to get them out first.'

Manny nodded. 'It's worth thinking about, but we've had generators running the whole day to make sure the creature doesn't feed on the townspeople, and it hasn't shown up at any of them. If we can't even attract the creature to a generator within city limits, how can we lure it all the way out to the army base?'

'I think I can explain that. I've theorised that the creature would be adversely affected by solar radiation since that wavelength of energy is significantly different from its own. I thought it would hibernate during the day, both to avoid sunlight and also to conserve energy. The last few days have basically proved my theory. All the incidents with the creature have happened at night, or at dawn or dusk, when solar radiation is a lot weaker. If we leave the electricity turned off in Carlton tonight, and turn on all the generators at the base, I'm sure the creature would go back there. Though I'd prefer to wipe it out, I have no idea how we could manage that. Trapping it is the next best option.'

Deciding Gavin was on the level, Manny quickly filled him in on their idea to destroy the creature in the town swimming pool.

'That sounds like a plan,' Gavin agreed. 'If you like I can go over to the pool and give them my technical expertise. There aren't very many people who know more about the creature than I do.'

'That would be great,' Manny said.

With no other words necessary, Gavin returned to his car in the hospital parking lot and set off for the centre of the city. Manny watched him go. Once Gavin's car had disappeared around the corner, Manny climbed into his jeep and started the engine. It was time for him to go back to the college.

Chapter 21

Just before five o'clock that afternoon, Manny drove his jeep towards the centre of the city. Carla had taken the passenger seat beside him, while Grace sat in the tray. The sky was mostly clear and a warm wind was blowing in from the desert. Manny had packed away the jeep's canopy, once again leaving the cab open to the air. All things considered, they couldn't ask for better conditions in which to attempt the pool plan.

As they neared the park they were stunned to see how many people had turned out to help. Both sides of the street were packed with cars. People were gathered on the sidewalk talking, as well as a few on the road itself. Yet more stood in doorways, and probably many others were currently inside. All three in the jeep knew just how dangerous the creature was, but had obviously failed to impress that fact on everyone else.

'Looks like we'll have to walk from here,' Grace said, eyeing the mass of cars in front of them.

Realising she was right, Manny pulled into the first vacant space he could find. As soon as the jeep had come to a stop, Grace climbed out of the tray. She was surprised to see that a nearby car was unlocked with the keys in the ignition. Then it made sense. If something went wrong, people would be desperate to escape. Leaving the keys meant anyone in need could use the car. She guessed most of the vehicles on the block were the same. When Manny left his keys as well, Grace decided someone must have arranged it.

After getting out of the jeep and closing the door, Manny glanced down to check his watch. Sunset was only a few minutes away and he wanted to make sure everything was proceeding to plan. With the girls following closely behind, he started along the street, instinctively looking around for anything that might cause a problem.

The pool was situated close to the intersection, within a complex that also held the grandstands, locker rooms and a small shop. Normally these would be separated from the rest of the park by a chain-link fence, but during the day someone had removed it, probably to ensure there was no barrier between the creature and the pool.

A gazebo sat in the centre of the park. It was octagonal in shape, and stood about a metre off the ground. At the base of the structure Manny could see a small hatch, and knew that behind it was a generator and a collection of lights which could be set up for night-time celebrations. Though the lights were currently packed away, when in position they were powerful enough to illuminate most of the park.

The generator they would be using for the operation sat on a raft by the edge of the pool. Several engineering students were gathered around it making their final checks. Gavin Powell was there too, clearly in charge of the group. Once the generator was ready, ropes connected to the raft would be used to pull it to the centre of the pool where it could be secured in place. From that point on the only way for the creature to reach it would be to go through the water.

If it somehow managed to survive, feeding would be its first priority. To ensure the safety of everyone present, the alternate generators Manny had organised the night before were ready to go. With a single radio call one or more would be turned on in order to lure the creature away.

Confident that everything was going to plan, Manny allowed himself to relax a little. He glanced across the street and saw Charlotte standing with a group of college students. She had a bag in her hands and was passing out torches and bottles of water. Manny sent Carla and Grace over to confer with her, while he continued into the park to where a tent had been erected. It would serve as a command post until the sun went down. At that point all the personnel would gather on top of the various multi-storey buildings located nearby.

Manny found the person in charge of the operation. Her name was Rebecca Channon. She was studying advanced physics, chemistry and biology, making her well qualified for the position.

'What's our status?' Manny asked.

'Everything is ready. We have the generator by the pool. The engineering students are checking it over as we speak. One of the technicians from the army is here too, giving us a hand. We'll switch the generator on and put it in the pool once the sun has set. The army guy, I think his name is Gavin, told us the creature is more active at night, probably something to do with solar energy during the day. Doing this after dark should increase our chance of success.'

'Makes sense,' Manny agreed.

'As sunset approaches, everyone will move into the buildings. We also have people spread across town. If the creature appears somewhere else, we can try to lead it in this direction. But because the electricity is off everywhere else, we're fairly certain as soon as we start the generator it will come straight here. The generator is the most powerful we could find in the time we had, so the creature is sure to sense it.'

'Sounds like you have everything under control.'

Manny looked towards the horizon as the sun began to disappear behind the mountains. Darkness descended over the town faster than anyone expected.

Gavin and the students inspecting the generator finished their final checks and gave Manny the all-clear. Most of the group headed for the rooftops leaving Gavin alone beside the generator.

'Is everything else ready?' he asked Manny.

'That's it,' Manny said, then turned to the remaining spectators and told them to retreat to a safer place. The buildings were close enough that they would easily be able to see what was happening, but not so close as to be in any danger.

Manny and Gavin waited until everyone else had made their way indoors, then Gavin stood aside and allowed Manny to start the generator. Together they pushed the raft into the water. Using the ropes they dragged it to the centre of the pool and secured it in place.

There was nothing to do now but wait.

Chapter 22

On top of a three storey building across from the pool, Carla and Grace sat together on a blanket provided by Charlotte. They watched as Manny started the generator then made his way inside. Carla saw the worry in Grace's eyes, even though the creature was nowhere around.

'He's a big boy,' Carla consoled. 'He can look after himself.'

'That may have been true a few weeks ago, before the creature arrived, but now I'm not so sure.'

'You could be right. But as long as we stick together we'll be able to work through this.'

'Are you really sure this is the time to pep-talk me?' Grace asked her.

'It's as much for me as it is for you,' Carla replied ruefully. She hadn't planned on being so honest.

Grace glanced around at the other people on the roof. All of them looked like they wanted to be somewhere else. A few were taking the time to catch up on some much-needed studying, but mostly they sat in small groups, talking softly and trying not to imagine how things could go wrong.

Given that she had been one of the driving forces behind the pool plan, Grace felt more on edge than any of them. If something bad happened, the responsibility would rest firmly on her shoulders.

Her thoughts were interrupted as Manny and Gavin arrived on the roof. They were immediately approached by a group of students wanting confirmation that everything was still going to plan.

Grace watched them for a moment.

'What's his deal?' she asked Carla.

'Who, Manny?'

'Yeah. He acts so strange sometimes.'

'In what regard?'

'He seems to run hot and cold. One minute he wants me around, the next it's like he's trying to get rid of me.'

'Aren't you exaggerating a little?'

'I wish I was. Yesterday morning he invited me to breakfast, but the next minute he was handing me off to Charlotte so he could go looking for the creature. The same thing happened at the mall when he went after the guy we saw from the roof even though he would have been better off with an extra set of eyes. Or what about early this morning, when he chose to go to the army base alone.'

'He was trying to protect you. That's just the way he is. He knew if you went with him he might not be able to ensure your safety.'

'Does he date much?' Grace asked, sounding more interested than she intended.

'Not really. I think a lot of girls assume there's something going on between him and I, but that's not the case. Mostly he's just too busy. He has school, work and volunteering at the hospital. There aren't enough hours in the day for him to do everything that needs to be done. But I think for the right girl he'd find the time.'

Carla climbed to her feet, pretending she needed to confer with Charlotte. Really she was giving Grace some time alone to think.

Like the previous nights, with the sun gone the temperature began to fall. Grace pulled her jacket tighter, trying to conserve what little warmth remained. All around her other students were doing the same thing. A few had even drifted indoors to escape the cold.

On the far side of the building Manny was staring intently down at the pool. Gavin and the others had wandered off, leaving him alone, though Grace doubted he would stay that way for long. She decided to take advantage of his solitude and crossed the roof to speak to him.

Manny smiled as she approached, and seemed genuinely happy she had come over.

'How long do you think we'll have to wait?' Grace asked.

'I don't know. This generator is the only source of electricity in town. The creature should definitely be on its way.' He shrugged, pretending to be unconcerned. 'I wish it would hurry up. I want to see if this idea will work.'

'What will we do if it doesn't show?'

'If we miss our chance tonight I think the best thing we can do is to try again tomorrow, though Colonel Markham thinks the army will have returned by then. Still, if we keep things low-key, we might be able to do it without attracting their attention.'

They drifted off into a comfortable silence for a minute. Grace used a flashlight to check her watch. Already more than ten minutes had passed since Manny started the generator.

'It should have been here by now,' she said. 'Maybe it's not coming.'

'Don't worry,' Manny said. 'No-one reported seeing it today at the other generators we set up, and we turned off the army's generator early this morning, so we can assume it hasn't had anything to eat since then. That's more than twelve hours without any food. My guess is it's feeling pretty hungry by now.'

'Then why hasn't it appeared?'

'It's probably just being cautious after of almost getting caught last night.'

Manny looked towards the horizon. With the exception of the previous night, it was the first time in a long while that he had seen the city appear so dark and desolate. Even late at night there were usually a few lights still on somewhere. He took comfort in the knowledge that no-one was inadvertently attracting the creature by using electricity.

'This is a new experience for me,' Grace said, interrupting his chain of thought.

'What part are you referring to?'

'Everything. Running between rooftops, ditching my studies, chasing a monster around the city. I'm not sure my parents would approve.'

'You're helping out the people of this town. Just pretend it's some sort of extra-curricular activity. If you're lucky you might even be able to get extra credit for it,' he joked.

'If this is just another class, I can't wait for the final assessment.'

Manny smiled. 'You're doing well. Better than most people.'

He surveyed the rooftop. Half the people were keeping watch for the creature, but a lot of the others were reading by torchlight. 'You should have brought some homework with you. At least then the time wouldn't be a total waste.'

'I don't think I would get much work done even if I had brought some stuff. There's just too much on my mind.'

She would have continued, but suddenly there was a loud whistle from the far corner of the building. Grace looked at Manny. 'It's here,' she said.

Along with everyone else they rushed to the side of the roof, jockeying for a position by the edge where they could have a clear view of what was happening.

The creature approached from the north, adding weight to the theory it had been hibernating in the warehouse district. Though it had been half a day without food, it didn't seem in any hurry to reach the generator.

Grace held her breath. Everything they had worked for over the past twelve hours rested on the next few moments.

The creature crossed the road and headed into the park.

It reached the edge of the pool and scrutinised the area, contemplating its options. Considering the events of the previous night, its caution was understandable.

Suddenly, without any warning at all, it jumped towards the generator. It sailed in a high arc, seemingly moving in slow motion. In that instant Grace had the overwhelming fear it would reach the raft.

There was a splash as the creature's hindquarters made contact with the water, but its front feet landed on the platform. It struggled frantically for several seconds, trying to pull itself up, but all to no avail. The raft wobbled as the creature slipped below the waves.

From one of the nearby rooftops, someone turned off the generator using a remote control. People began to shine spotlights down from the buildings, all aimed at the spot where the creature had disappeared.

Minutes passed without any sign of it and everyone started to relax. Everyone except Manny. He continued to stare at the pool, searching for absolute confirmation that the creature had been killed. He assumed there would be some sort of massive energy release, perhaps an explosion, but nothing like that occurred. He realised he would have to go down there. It wasn't something he wanted to do, even though there was no sign that the creature was still alive, but he didn't have any other option.

'Stay on the buildings,' he said into his radio. 'I'll see if I can figure out what's happened.'

He ran down the fire-escape, then crossed the road and approached the pool. Carla and Grace watched with trepidation.

'Anything?' asked a voice on all the radios.

'I don't see it. There are ripples all over the place, but even if there weren't, I don't think it would make a difference. It's transparent, just like the water,' Manny said.

'What do you want to do?' returned the voice.

'I don't know. I guess we can try starting the generator again. If the creature's under the water, we may be able to entice it up to the surface, and if it somehow managed to leave the area without being seen, it might still be nearby. If it lost a lot of energy, it will have no choice but to come back to replenish itself.'

'Okay. I'll start it with the remote.'

'No, I'll do it. I want to make sure there's no water on the generator. Otherwise it might short-circuit. Keep watch for the creature just in case. If it's still alive I don't want it sneaking up on me.'

He ran around the side of the pool and untied the ropes that held the raft in place, then pulled it to the edge. Though the platform was covered with water, the generator was dry and sprang to life as soon as Manny turned the key.

Quickly he manoeuvred the raft back to the centre of the pool and secured it in place once more.

Rather than return to the roof, Manny entered the small shop next to the pool and waited by the front counter. Looking through the windows he had an unobstructed view of the pool and off into the park. Though the kiosk was less secure than its multi-storey counterparts, it provided a better view since it was so much closer to the action. If the creature was still alive and anywhere nearby, Manny was guaranteed to see it.

Chapter 23

Five minutes later, with no sign that the creature had survived, Manny radioed the person with the remote and told them to shut off the generator. A moment later the air fell silent.

'Now what?' the voice asked.

'I guess the best thing to do is send everyone home. I might stick around here and try the generator again in an hour or so. But I think if the creature was still alive it would have made an appearance by now.'

Suddenly there was movement all around. People abandoned their positions on the roofs and raced downstairs, but rather than going home, they crossed the road towards the pool, eager to see for themselves that the creature was really gone.

Manny wanted to believe it was over just as much as everyone else, but he couldn't shake the feeling of dread that seemed to rise from the pit of his stomach. Though there was no sign of the creature, neither was there any proof that it had been destroyed. He left the shop and headed for the approaching group.

Cheers sounded in the night. Someone had brought a cooler out of the buildings and was passing around drinks. Lights shining from the roofs were no longer aimed at the spot where the creature had disappeared, but instead were pointed to the paved area nearby, where people were starting to gather. Grace had followed the throng down from upstairs, but now watched the celebration feeling somehow separate from it. She was sharing the same dread as Manny. She looked back to the doorway she had just left, hoping to see Carla.

Someone handed Manny a drink. He turned to give it back, but the person had already faded into the crowd. He tried to tell those around him to forget the party and go home, but no-one was listening. They all believed the creature was dead.

Manny stood by the edge of the pool, not knowing what to do, or even if anything needed to be done.

As he tried to figure out what was causing his sense of impending doom, some movement in the pool caught his attention. Something strange was happening, but he couldn't quite figure out what it was. Then it struck him. Even though there was no wind, small ripples were spreading from the centre of the pool out to the edge.

Manny knew what was coming next. He frantically glanced around, trying to see if anyone else had noticed, but they were all too caught up in the impromptu party. Then suddenly Grace was beside him. Somehow she had known he needed her.

'We have to get everyone out of here,' she said. She wasn't looking at the pool but he knew she had seen it too. She spoke quietly, trying not to alarm the people nearby, aware that a panic would make things even worse.

A loud roar filled the air. The revelry stopped immediately. Everyone looked nervously from side to side, trying to figure out what was happening. Someone by the pool gasped as a claw broke through the surface of the water. It was still mostly transparent, but seemed more solid now than ever. The talons grabbed for the edge of the raft. In one smooth movement the creature pulled itself onto the platform, at the same time splashing water all over the generator.

Grace looked to Manny to see what he wanted to do. He wished she hadn't. He was as much out of his depth as she. The rest of the people assembled were more decisive. Almost everyone took off running away from the creature and towards the safety of the buildings. A few stood too shocked to move, but with every passing second, more realised fleeing was the only sensible option. In the panic to leave, several people fell. Some were helped up, others hindered by the mass of people rushing past.

From the edge of the group, closer to the buildings than anyone else, Carla saw what was happening. She had no ideas, no plan, only that she had to reach Manny's side. She was aware it was a suicidal notion, but if she left him and he needed help she would regret it for the rest of her life. She dodged through the crowd, carefully avoiding contact with everyone so they couldn't push her back. She made it to Manny and Grace as they started backing away. Manny almost tripped over her. He shot her a look halfway between anger and thankfulness.

'Any ideas?' she asked, knowing he had none.

He shook his head, his face a mask of fear. The creature stared at them from on the raft but didn't move. From the moment it had clawed its way out of the water, barely thirty seconds previously, it had eyes only for Manny and the two girls. Maybe, somewhere deep in whatever it had for a mind, it remembered them.

Without warning it jumped towards them, leaping from the raft, over the water and onto dry land in a single bound.

Now it stood only a few metres away. Manny knew they were out of time. But not out of luck.

The generator sprang to life. Manny didn't bother to wonder how or why. The creature was momentarily distracted. Then, sparks flew as the generator short-circuited from the water dropped on it only moments before.

Manny ran, dragging the two girls behind him. After a few steps Carla stumbled. He turned to help her up. Grace stopped several paces further on. He appreciated the gesture but didn't need her to be a hero.

'Run,' he yelled.

She took off for the end of the street, where the cars were parked.

Manny pulled Carla to her feet. His eyes darted from side to side as he tried to think of the best course of action. He looked into the park. Even in the darkness he could see the gazebo. An idea sprang into his head. He wasn't sure how well it would work, but it would buy everyone at least a few more moments to escape. He started running towards the structure. The instant he changed direction Carla understood his plan.

The creature turned back to Manny and Carla, but in the confusion they had managed to escape. It started towards a group of college students, some of the last to leave. They were running for the buildings but would never make it in time.

Grace arrived beside Manny's jeep, but before she could get in she was struck by an idea. She leaned through the window of the neighbouring car and turned the key. The engine sprang to life. It was a gamble, but perhaps the energy would distract the creature long enough to allow her to get to Manny and Carla.

Quickly Grace climbed behind the wheel of the jeep. She looked up in time to see the creature knock down one of the people it had been chasing. But it didn't pass through them. Instead they were pushed violently out of the way. Even from this distance Grace could tell that being immersed in the pool had made the creature much more solid.

As the creature sensed the energy given off by the car it gave up its pursuit and turned towards Grace.

The student who had been knocked to the ground climbed to his feet and began moving painfully away. A moment later another student was by his side, helping him to safety. The encounter had obviously injured the person a great deal but the fact he could still walk was a good sign. Grace wondered briefly whether the young man had been injured by the creature's touch or as he made hard contact with the ground after being shoved aside. Either way, it was proof that an encounter with the creature was no longer fatal. But that didn't mean the danger was over.

Without a second to lose, she slipped the jeep into gear and started the engine, then pulled out of the parking space and sped back towards the creature. She roared past, missing it by only a few metres.

She saw Manny and Carla heading into the park. They weren't fleeing, but instead were moving purposefully towards the gazebo. Grace twisted the steering wheel and set the jeep on an interception course. She mounted the curb, cut across the park and pulled to a stop a few metres ahead of them, right beside the shelter.

'Get in,' she called.

Manny shook his head. 'Help us.'

Grace had no idea what he was talking about, but she left the jeep and ran to his side. Manny knelt down at the base of the gazebo. There was a small hatch there, but it was secured by a padlock. He started ripping at the wooden panels beside the door. He pried three loose and Grace was finally able to see a small generator and a string of lights.

'When we switch this on the creature will be distracted again,' Carla explained.

'Does it have fuel?' Grace asked.

Manny pulled off the fuel cap and checked the tank.

'It's half-full,' he said. He had no idea how long they would have to keep the creature busy for in order to ensure everyone was able to get to safety, but hoped half a tank would give them the advantage they needed.

'How much time do we have?' Carla asked.

Grace looked back at the creature. It was still at the car she had started, but the engine was no longer running. The creature had drained all the energy out of the battery in an attempt to reach its former capacity.

'Not long,' she said.

Manny found the switch but paused before he could hit it. His original intention had been to start the generator and use the energy to distract the creature so that everyone nearby could escape. But then he had a better idea.

He pulled the generator out of its enclosure and began loading it onto the back of the jeep. Grace did the same with the string of lights. For a moment Carla had no idea what they were doing, then it struck her. When they drove away the creature would sense the energy given off by the generator and come following after them, allowing everyone present even more time to flee.

As soon as the equipment was safely in the tray, Manny hopped into the driver's seat and started the engine. Carla sat beside him. Grace climbed into the back and quickly connected the lights to the generator, then flipped the switch. The machine roared to life. The string of lights immediately illuminated the area. Further along the street the creature turned to look in their direction. Manny was watching too, and as soon as he knew they had garnered its interest, he set off.

Chapter 24

'Where are we going?' Grace asked as they raced across the park with the creature in pursuit.

'We'll lead it away from the heart of the city, into a less populated area. That should allow everyone here enough time to get to safety,' Carla explained.

Manny focused mostly on the path ahead, but continued to check the rear-vision mirror to gauge how far he was from the creature. He could have easily outran it in the jeep, but he wanted to stay close enough that it wouldn't be distracted by anything else. He left the park and turned onto the main street of Carlton, then headed for the industrial district.

'I'm not sure if leading it away will be enough,' Manny said. 'Now that the creature's changed, we have no idea what it's capable of. It could be more dangerous than ever.'

'I don't think so,' Grace interrupted. 'I saw it hit into someone. They weren't seriously hurt. It was like they were just pushed out of the way.' She looked back towards the creature. It had fallen further behind, but was still following them. The increase in distance didn't dispel her unease.

Manny was perplexed. 'It's as though it's more solid now. It definitely looked that way coming out of the pool.'

'Actually,' said Carla, 'it makes sense. When it was in the pool, the water was draining all its energy. I think it developed a thicker skin in order to hold all the energy in.'

'That could be right,' Manny admitted, 'but we don't know if it's a permanent thing. It might already be reverting back to the way it was.'

'So what do you suggest?' Grace broke in. She knew dwelling on hypotheticals wouldn't get them anywhere.

'I have an idea,' Carla said. 'We can lead it out to the emergency generator at the airport. All that energy should easily keep it busy until morning. In the meantime, we can get everyone together and figure out what to do.'

'Starting the airport's generator and getting away clean could be a problem,' Manny said. 'It gives off a lot more energy than the generator we have. The creature will go straight for it as soon as it's turned on. Whoever starts it might not have enough time to escape.'

'If you drop me off right by the generator shed and lead the creature away, I can wait a few seconds, start the generator then run for the storage shed. If you and the creature are far enough away, I should have plenty of time to get to safety,' Carla volunteered.

As the two in the front seat continued to discuss the specifics of the idea, Grace checked on the creature again. It was gone. She looked frantically from side to side trying to locate it.

'Be quiet,' she commanded the others. They looked back at her, not understanding what was going on. 'It's not following us anymore.'

They were shocked to realise she was right. 'Where is it?' Manny asked.

'I don't know. I got distracted listening to the plan. When I looked back, I couldn't see it.'

'We need to find it before it's able to do any real damage,' Carla said pointlessly.

Grace was confused. 'Why did it stop following us? This generator is the only source of electricity in the whole town.'

'Maybe someone else started one,' Manny suggested. He glanced at Carla. 'Get on the radio and tell everyone to make sure all the other generators are turned off. Let them know we're going to lure the creature to the airport.'

As Carla pulled a walkie-talkie from her pocket and started to speak into it, Manny slowed the jeep, hoping that if the creature was nearby they would have a better chance of spotting it.

'We're not going to find it like this,' Grace said, 'and we're putting ourselves in more danger by driving around not knowing where it is.'

Carla finished her call, then tucked the radio back into her pocket and tried to be rational. 'Maybe we should return to where we lost it. We could...'

She was cut short by a tremendous noise as the creature charged out of a nearby alleyway. It was barely a metre away from them. Grace pulled herself to the far side of the jeep, putting as much distance between herself and the beast as possible, all the while scrambling to find something to repel it.

Suddenly it lunged at the jeep, hitting with a heavy thud and lifting two wheels off the ground. Manny pulled hard at the steering wheel, getting as close to the edge of the road as he dared, but he couldn't go any further without mounting the curb and rolling the jeep. If that happened they would be in even greater danger.

The creature charged again. Grace picked up the string of lights from the floor beside her and hurled them over the back of the jeep. Sparks flew as the lights hit the creature. It drew back as if stung. The lights shattered as they hit the ground, then trailed along uselessly behind the jeep, still connected to the generator by a thin cable.

Manny used the opportunity to pull further away from the creature. Grace kept her eyes on it, just to be sure it couldn't attempt another vanishing act. Though most of the lights were now shattered, she quickly dragged them back aboard the jeep. They had repelled the creature once, perhaps they would again.

'What happened?' Carla asked. 'The electricity seemed to hurt it.'

'I guess it has to do with the creature's thicker skin. In its old form, if it absorbed too much electricity, it could easily release the excess, but now it can't. It must have filled up on that car at the pool,' Manny explained.

'But if it's full, why is it still chasing us?'

'I guess we got it mad.'

That worried Grace, and not because of the extra danger they were now in, but because it threatened their plan. 'How do we get it to stay at the airport if it's chasing us? Our idea only works if it focuses on the generator. I don't want to hang around the desert until morning trying to keep it busy.'

'Even with thick skin, it will lose a lot of energy from chasing us. When we arrive at the airport and start the generator, the creature should go straight for it to replenish itself,' Manny guessed. 'We can use that time to escape. If we're not there to draws its focus, it should stay close to the generator.'

He glanced back to check the creature's position, at the same time moving the jeep back to the centre of the road. In the tray two broken lights nudged together, creating a shower of sparks. Grace shrieked in surprise, then kicked the wires apart, trying not to get electrocuted in the process.

Suddenly a thought occurred to Carla. She remembered the creature's reaction when Grace threw the string of lights at it, as well as what Manny had said about the thick skin stopping it from expelling excess energy. 'We can kill this thing,' she whispered, amazed at the sheer thought of the idea.

'What do you mean?' Manny asked.

'If we put enough electricity into the creature, it will overcharge, just like the torch Cameron was using last night.'

'Are you sure?'

'No, but at the moment it's the best chance we have.'

The logical part of Manny told him it was a bad idea, but the rest of him trusted Carla's judgement. 'What's your plan?' he asked.

'The generator at the airport is huge. It's probably a hundred times more powerful than the one we were using tonight. If I can increase the output enough, the creature should overload as soon as it makes contact,' Carla said. 'All the electricity will pour into it, and with its thicker skin, it won't be able to get rid of it.'

'How long will it take to reconfigure the generator?' Grace asked, looking back to ensure they were still being followed.

'Maybe ten minutes. It'll be up to you two to keep the creature distracted while I work.'

'It's too risky to have you trying to modify the generator with the creature nearby,' Grace said. 'If it came for you, you'd be trapped. What if you take a separate car to the airport, and we follow a few minutes later? Meanwhile, we'll keep the creature busy among the warehouses. I think that's the safest place.'

'That could work,' Carla agreed.

Compensating for the change in their plan, Manny altered his course a little, now heading for Carla's house so she could pick up her car. When they were a block away he sped up. He wanted to put more distance between the jeep and the creature so Carla would have a few extra seconds to safely disembark.

Grace checked her watch. 'We'll give you a fifteen minute head start. Good luck.'

'You too.'

Manny pulled to an abrupt stop directly in front of Carla's house. She jumped out of the jeep, ran across the yard and climbed behind the wheel of her car, then quickly manoeuvred out of the drive and down a side street. After ensuring the creature was still chasing the jeep, Manny set off once more.

Chapter 25

Twenty minutes later, after receiving the call from Carla telling them to start on their way, Manny and Grace drove through the desert towards the airport.

Manny kept his eyes on the road, a necessity because it was in such poor condition, while Grace watched the creature running along in the desert behind them. For the time being it seemed satisfied to stay clear of the jeep and she took comfort in that.

After what seemed like an eternity, the control tower came into view on the horizon. Grace allowed herself a sigh of relief. It was almost over.

'Tell Carla we're nearly there,' Manny instructed. 'With any luck she has the generator running by now.'

Grace pulled a walkie-talkie from her pocket and put it to her lips. 'We're less than two minutes away, Carla. The creature is right with us at the moment. How are you doing with the generator? Over.'

'I'm working on removing the surge protectors. It's not as easy as I was hoping but it should be ready by the time the two of you arrive.'

Carla didn't say anything else, so Grace assumed she had returned to the job at hand. Grace looked over at Manny. He was still focused on the road ahead of them, but she knew he had monitored the conversation.

For the rest of the journey the two in the jeep maintained a thoughtful silence, each painfully aware of all the things that could go wrong. Finally, with the creature still following close behind, they passed through the front gate of the airport.

Carla's car was tucked away behind the generator shed, and through the open doorway, light from a torch was visible, evidence that she was yet to finish her work.

'Keep going,' Grace said to Manny. 'I don't think Carla's ready yet.'

Doing as she asked, Manny steered around the buildings and out onto the runway. Suddenly, the lights from the jeep revealed a deep hollow just ahead. Manny tried to take evasive action but it was too late. The jeep slammed into the hole, twisting the front wheels and guiding the car off the airstrip with enough speed to force it partly into a drainage channel directly in front of the control tower. Manny immediately knew the jeep wouldn't be going anywhere else that night.

He unbuckled his seatbelt and turned to help Grace with hers, then together they climbed from the jeep. The creature stood about thirty metres away, watching them intently. On a night when so much had gone wrong, it was a comfort to know they weren't completely out of luck. If it had taken this opportunity to attack, they would have both been goners.

'What's the plan?' Grace asked Manny, keeping her eyes on the creature and her voice low.

'We need to get to the buildings without it coming after us. Then all we have to do is wait for Carla to start the generator.' He took Grace by the hand and they slowly backed away.

The creature seemed torn between following them or going for the generator, but finally ambled over to the jeep. Manny and Grace took advantage of the distraction and hurried towards the storage shed.

As Grace entered she was immediately struck by a feeling of emptiness. A bank of windows allowed light from the almost full moon to enter, making the vacant space in front of her look even more unearthly.

In the centre of the room, beside the staircase, a metal support reached up to the ceiling. Attached to the post was a switch, probably for the lights. It didn't appear to be in good condition. All the wires had melted together, and it seemed as though it had been that way for some time.

Manny and Grace quickly ascended to the second floor and positioned themselves at windows on opposite sides of the room. Manny looked towards the generator shed hoping to see some indication Carla had completed her part of the plan, while Grace scanned the area in the direction of the jeep, trying to reacquire sight of the creature. Unfortunately, even with the moonlight, she was unable to catch a glimpse of it.

Manny pulled a radio from his pocket and spoke into it.

'We've arrived, Carla, but I crashed the jeep. The sooner you finish up, the better. We're waiting in the storage shed. The creature's around somewhere too, but we can't see it.'

Carla's voice came over the line. 'I'm almost done. I'll meet you there.'

'See you soon,' Manny said, sliding the radio back into his pocket.

Almost immediately he heard the generator start. At the same time a strange buzzing filled the air and he realised it was the electricity running through all the old cables. A moment later he saw Carla exit the generator shed. He watched through the second floor windows as she ran towards the storage shed, then went downstairs, ready to greet her as she came through the door. Grace followed a few steps behind.

Carla entered the room with a smile on her face. 'The generator is running at full capacity. All we have to do now is wait.'

'We can keep watch from the second floor,' Manny said. 'That way we'll be able to see exactly what happens.'

He reached out to take Carla's hand, but suddenly froze, all the blood draining from his face. By his expression, Carla knew exactly what was happening. She didn't bother to turn and look. She pushed off with all her strength, trying to put some distance between herself and the creature.

It moved fast and caught her before she had taken her first step, grabbing her by the shoulders and lifting her into the air. For a second it stood on two legs. Then, with all the force it could muster, it threw Carla into the wall.

Manny had no idea what to do, only that he had to reach Carla before the creature could cause any more harm. He tried to move but Grace held him firm. She knew going to Carla's aid would only get them all killed. Instead she dragged him backwards and started shoving him up the stairs, at the same time reaching for the switch on the central support. Sparks flew as she slammed it downwards. With nothing more she could do to distract the creature, Grace followed Manny up to the second level. They turned as they reached the top.

Carla still lay on the floor, unmoving, but the creature was no longer interested in her. As Manny and Grace watched in horror, it did something they weren't expecting. It put its front foot on the stairs and started to climb.

With fleeing their only option, the two hurried onto the external deck of the storage shed. Together they pushed the old door shut, knowing it wouldn't buy them much time.

'It's not going for the generator,' Grace exclaimed. 'It must have replenished its energy at the jeep.'

Manny didn't seem to hear her. 'I have to get to Carla,' he said.

Grace nodded. 'We can take the other door. Sneak in, get her out and be gone before it knows what happened.'

'I'll do it. You hide in the control tower. You'll be safe there.'

There wasn't time for argument. Grace hurried across the catwalk as Manny raced down the external stairs. On the deck of the control tower, Grace was surprised to see Manny's telescope. It felt like months since they had left it there, rather than just two days.

She entered the control room and rushed to the windows in time to see Manny vanish inside the ground floor entrance of the storage shed. She held her breath as she waited for him to reappear with Carla.

Almost immediately Manny backed out of the doorway, but he didn't have Carla with him. A moment later the creature followed him out. It had stopped chasing them up the stairs and had decided to use the other exit.

Instinctively Grace scanned the room for some way to aid Manny's escape. On the wall beside her was an old fire-axe. She had no idea what damage, if any, it would do to the creature. Aside from the axe, the only objects nearby were a few old chairs that would be even less helpful.

She saw a row of flashing lights on one of the control panels, and realised that with the generator on, all the airport's systems had become active. Desperate to distract the creature, she flipped every switch she could find.

The lights on the runway flickered to life, then a second later the whole complex was further illuminated. Outside the window, the buzzing of the power cables seemed to double.

Manny turned towards the control tower, his attention caught by the noise from the wires. Through the window he could see Grace standing beside the fire-axe, frantically searching for some way to help.

He looked back at the creature. It hadn't been distracted by the lights. He glanced at Grace one last time. Then suddenly his expression changed. It wasn't fear that etched itself across his features, but hope. He pointed up.

It took Grace a moment to figure out what he meant.

Attached to the building, just to the side of the windows, were two rusted and decaying electric cables. She traced the path of the wires, from outside the control room to the first floor doorway of the storage building, right above the creature's head. She remembered how Manny had mentioned the cables when they arrived at the airport two days earlier, thinking they wouldn't be much good because they would soon break. How wrong he was. Now she was counting on that weakness.

She wasted a second looking for the latch on the window. There wasn't one. The window was designed to stay permanently closed. She picked up a nearby chair and swung with all her might, shattering the glass with one blow. She released the chair and let it fall outside the building.

Manny didn't turn to look as it hit the ground behind him. Grace wanted him to run, to get as far away as he possibly could, but for the idea to work he had to keep the creature occupied for a few extra seconds. Grace pulled her eyes away from the scene below and focused on the fire-axe. It was in a cabinet behind a thin sheet of glass. With no time to waste she pulled the sleeve of her jacket over her hand and struck out at the pane, causing it to shatter. She flicked a few loose shards out of the way then grabbed the axe.

She looked through the window and tried to judge the best angle to strike. There was only time for one shot. She pulled the axe back and then swung it forward, almost cutting the line. A few strands of tiny, twisted wire remained. The creature charged at Manny. Under the weight of the cable the remaining strands snapped. Manny heard the rush of wind as the line fell and saw the creature darting towards him. He dived to the side. The wire slammed into the creature before it could cut the distance between Manny and itself in half. It started to vibrate as the energy from the cable was transferred into its body. Sparks flew in every direction.

Grace wanted to believe the energy from one line would be enough to destroy the creature, but she couldn't take the chance. She swung at the other cable. Either her second hit was stronger than the first, or the remaining line was weaker. The axe cut through the wire with one stroke. It fell towards the creature, hitting it straight on. Grace dropped the axe and looked down at Manny. He had pulled himself to his feet and was standing transfixed by the spectacle. The creature was shivering and beginning to glow. It started humming, getting louder and louder until it was almost unbearable. Grace knew it wasn't over yet.

She put her hands on windowsill and launched herself through the opening, ignoring the pain as shards of glass bit into her flesh. She landed on a thin ledge that ran along the edge of the building, then dropped to the ground a few steps from Manny. The hum from the creature became an ear-splitting trill. Grace dived at Manny and tackled him. They landed behind a pile of discarded crates. The creature exploded. A wave of hot energy passed over them both. Grace helped Manny to his feet.

The creature was gone. In its place were dark scorch marks. The intense heat had burned the ground where it had stood only moments before. The surrounding area was littered with little blobs of what looked like clear jelly, but was actually the pure, solidified energy the creature had been made up of.

As Manny and Grace watched, the blobs sparkled in the bright airport lighting. After a few seconds they seemed to fade away until nothing of the creature remained.

'What now?' Grace asked.

Before Manny could reply, there was a sound from the second floor of the storage shed.

'Stay here,' he said.

Grace didn't reply, but when he moved forward, she followed.

They both stopped in surprise as Carla limped around the side of the building and started slowly and painfully descending the stairs. She stumbled as she reached the bottom step, but Manny was fast enough to catch her as she fell.

'How are you doing?' he asked gently.

'I'm fine,' she said, attempting a casual smile. It froze halfway across her face. 'Actually, I think I may have cracked some ribs.' She took a few steps then doubled over in pain.

'We need to get you to a hospital,' Manny said rather obviously. 'Get the jeep,' he instructed Grace, forgetting for a moment that it was still in a ditch beside the runway. Grace nodded and hurried away.

'What about the creature?' asked Carla.

'It's dead.'

'Was that the noise I heard?' Without waiting for his reply she asked, 'How did you manage that?'

'Grace cut the power-lines connecting the storage shed and the control tower. When they hit the creature, it exploded.'

Grace returned moments later with Carla's car and together with Manny gently helped Carla into the front seat. Manny went around to the driver's door as Grace climbed into the back.

Carla winced in pain as she slipped on her seatbelt. Though she was putting on a tough front, Manny wanted to get her to the hospital as quickly as possible. He found it hard to believe she was still standing after the pummelling she had received.

As he pulled away from the buildings, Manny looked to the east. It didn't matter that sunrise was still over eight hours away. It would be a beautiful morning.

Grace leaned forward from the back seat of Carla's car. 'There's one thing I've been meaning to ask you, Manny.'

'What's that?' he asked.

'What do people do for fun around here?'

'There's a cinema. I like to go to the afternoon screenings. Tuesday is half-price.'

'Would you like to go to a movie with me on Tuesday?'
Grace asked.

Manny smiled easily; confidently. 'Tuesday is good,' he
said, 'but tomorrow would be even better.'

####

About The Author

Wayne Phillips lives in Queensland, Australia. His main focuses are fantasy, supernatural and science fiction, plus a little bit of mystery thrown in for good measure. Most days he spends procrastinating away from his computer, and at night he can be found frantically scribbling down any and all ideas that pop into his head.

If you enjoyed this book, please consider leaving a short review at your place of purchase.